# Bedtime Stories for Kids

## Stories for Children With Valuable Lessons (Goodnight Stories Collection)

## Tania Alagona

# Table of contents

# Introduction: Dedicated to all the children of the world

**Bedtime Stories for Kids:** Stories for Children With Valuable Lessons (Goodnight Stories Collection)

This book is dedicated to all the little boys and little girls who love to dream, those who feel like tireless travelers and voracious listeners. What better way to dream than through bedtime stories?

You may not believe this, but even the author of this book was once a little girl. Writing stories for children is the best way to become a child again!

Reading a story to our kids can easily become a great night-time habit, provided that we have the right support. Grown-ups can read this book, but it is also meant to be read by the most daring children: those who have just started learning how to read and those who are already doing well.

Remember to help your kids with sections they don't understand well. There are many benefits that can be derived from these stories. They establish a relationship with the parents' voice, promote relaxation before sleep, strengthen the child's imagination, and teach valuable lessons through the good deeds that the characters perform.

The best moment to read these stories is before going to bed, to promote a good night's rest and to nourish the dreams of our children or grandchildren. A story can be appreciated at any time of the day. Try it and I promise you won't regret it!

This book includes unique fairy tales and fables. They were specifically designed to create positive emotions and to help immerse both adults and children in the story.

These stories have a meaning and a moral, which are revealed at the end of each chapter. Some will be funny, others will make you think about life and everyday things, others again will immerse you in the characters.

We will learn together to respect all living beings, respect our environment, be kinder to others, and love diversity. When children become attached to characters, they learn the values taught by the story.

To the children: try to pay attention while you listen or read. All of these stories have some truth to them, which can be useful in your daily life. The lessons at the end of the stories are called morals.

All that's left is to wish you good imaginary travels!

# The Tree of Life

Once upon a time, in an ancient temple in China, there was a thousand-year-old tree guarded by panda monks. The tree was on the top of the hill where the monks gathered to pray, and to reach it you had to climb two thousand steps.

It was said that the fruits of this tree could give vigor and great strength to anyone who ate them.

For this reason, it was called the tree of life, and the powers its fruits gave were so famous, that travelers came from all over the world hoping to taste them.

However, the naive travelers didn't know that they would have to pay a price to obtain the privilege of eating the fruits. The panda monks imposed a strict rule on all those who wanted to venture into their temple.

"Whoever wishes to taste these fruits and possess their strength must obey what the pandas say, defeat them, and become stronger."

This was a big problem for many people because the pandas weren't just simple monks..... no no no, ladies and gentlemen, these monks guarded the most secret and powerful martial art techniques in the world.

Many daring travelers tried to pass their tests, and the few who managed to do so became undefeated warriors. However, the tasks given by the monks were so tough, that the vast majority of people failed miserably.

"Go down two thousand steps and then climb up again without ever stopping!"

"Now go without food for three days, and then meditate for another seven without stopping!"

"Fight against three monks using only one hand!"

"Practice standing on your head until you no longer feel tiredness!"

Many regretted having ever made that journey because the monks were so strong and well-trained, and their requests were so absurd, that anyone who wanted to obtain the fruits quickly changed their mind.

Timo and Kiran arrived at the temple after many days of travel. They were two young people who had been looking for that place for a whole year, driven by the tales of adventurers.

"Oh panda monks, we greet you with reverence and humbly ask you to let us eat the fruits of the tree of life," they said, unaware of what was awaiting them.

However, the only reply they received was, "Whoever wishes to taste these fruits and possess their strength must obey what the pandas say, defeat them, and become stronger."

"The tree is at the top of this staircase. You may go see it now!"

So, the two climbed up the stairs, and they reached the top exhausted. Near the tree, a monk sat waiting for them, and when he saw them, he welcomed them with a big smile and said, "Congratulations, you did it! Now go down all the steps and tell the monk who sent you here that you managed to reach the top!"

Timo and Kiran, who were now desperate, went back down the two thousand steps, and once they reached the base of the stairs, the other monk congratulated them. Then he spoke to them once more with great kindness. "Since you're already here, could you bring these buckets of water up to the top to water the tree of life? I would be very grateful if you did that."

Thus, the two youths loaded the buckets on their back, and with great effort, climbed up all the steps until they reached the top of the hill, completely exhausted.

"Can we eat the fruits now?" Kiran asked the monk.

"Of course you can, no problem, but before that, you must defeat the monk who sent you here with the water. By the way, could you please carry these two stones down? They're needed to repair a part of the temple!" Concluded the panda.

When the two arrived at the base of the stairs, they no longer even had the strength to stand up. In fact, they couldn't even hit the panda monk once, who easily dodged all of their blows. This was the first of many trials that they had to face.

For weeks, Timo and Kiran woke up at dawn, and they obeyed everything that the monks told them to do until late at night. They had to stay still like statues for hours, meditate while balancing their bodies on sharp rocks, do without food, fight against the monks, practice running, and most of all, go up and down countless steps.

Six months passed this way, and although many travelers had given up already, Timo and Kiran never lost heart. On the contrary, they seemed to be enjoying the strange tasks that the monks gave them.

Then, finally one day, the impossible happened. The guardian monk of the tree was defeated in a fight. Timo and Kiran had managed to beat the panda, using their strength and their teamwork.

"Today, you defeated me! I don't have anything else to teach you, and if you want, you can now eat the fruit of the tree of life!" Announced the panda.

The two youths couldn't hold back their tears. After all that struggle, their efforts had finally been rewarded, and they could now obtain the strength and vigor they had dreamed of for so long.

However, once they finished eating the fruit, they were a little disappointed because they didn't notice any changes in their bodies.

"What is the meaning of this? Why isn't anything happening? Have you tricked us?" Timo shouted, convinced that he had just wasted a lot of time.

"Dear travelers, have you not come from so far to acquire strength and vigor?" Asked the panda.

"Of course! Why else would we have tolerated all of that strenuous torture?" Replied in unison the two travelers.

So, the monk gracefully walked up to them and said: "Didn't you notice how much you've improved in the last six months? Don't you realize that you've become strong? You even managed to defeat me, when at the beginning you couldn't even hit me!".

The two looked at each other and said: "Don't you mean to say that...?"

"Exactly," cut in the monk. "The fruits of the tree don't have anything special about them except for their delicious taste! You have acquired the strength that you sought through all the training you received in the temple!"

**MORAL:** Sometimes, we are promised easy gains in a short time. However, the truth is that to obtain good skills, you have to work hard. The easiest way to do that is to fall in love with the effort. If you can see effort as an enjoyable thing, then everything will seem less complicated.

# Pranks in the Forest

One morning like any other, in the forest, a turtle was about to wake up.

Something wasn't quite right, though. That morning was colder than usual and even if she stayed all curled up on herself, the turtle could still feel the chill on her wrinkly skin.

"My shell! My shell disappeared! Someone stole my precious shell! How will I protect myself now?" The poor animal who had lost her shelter complained loudly.

Not too far away, behind the bushes, near a big rock, someone was laughing triumphantly: "Ha ha ha ha! Did you see her face?" said a small voice.

"And all those wrinkles too! I almost died laughing!" replied another small voice. The turtle was too busy looking for her own shell to notice anything.

Meanwhile, in the same forest, a chameleon was also waking up, ready to go eat some insects as was his habit in the morning. When he tried to camouflage himself with his colors on the trunk of a tree, he noticed that the insects were all running away. He couldn't even catch one of them!

So, he tried changing color and he hid in the leaves, but the grasshoppers saw him anyway and ran away. The desperate chameleon realized that he couldn't change color anymore.

"My colors! My colors are gone! How am I going to hide in the vegetation now? How will I feed myself?" shouted the poor reptile desperately.

Meanwhile, on top of a tree, someone was laughing boisterously: "Ha ha ha ha! Did you see his face?" asked a small voice.

"Ha ha ha ha! The poor chameleon couldn't change color anymore!" replied another small voice.

The chameleon went to the fairy Olga to solve his problem since everyone went to her whenever something went wrong.

All of a sudden, a bear's screams were heard throughout the wood. Judging by how loudly he was shouting, he seemed very very angry.

"My honey stores.... they're gone! Someone stole all my honey last night and they did it while I was sleeping! If I find them, I will make them bitterly regret what they did!" The bear shouted while furiously looking for that sweet nectar.

Safe behind a large leaf, someone was savoring that divine food: "This honey is delicious. We should do this more often, shouldn't we?" asked a small voice, who was enjoying the loot.

"Of course! I already know where we should go tonight! By the way, did you see the bear's face? So funny!" replied the other small voice.

That morning many animals woke up with a start, and something strange had happened to all of them during the night. The forest was in a nervous mood and many animals were complaining.

The butterfly had woken up without any dust in her wings, and for that reason, she couldn't fly anymore. Then there was the boar whose nose had been stuffed with two acorns, stuck in the nostrils, and couldn't smell anymore.

The hedgehog's spikes had been cut and he couldn't defend himself from danger anymore. The squirrel had woken up painted all black and white, and now the other animals avoided him because they thought he was a skunk!

The situation had become unbearable. After all, this wasn't the first time that strange things happened in the morning. Strange pranks had been happening for some time involving many of the forest animals, as if someone found it amusing to see others struggle.

That morning in particular, the fairy Olga was overwhelmed by all the furious animals' complaints and demands.

"Look what they did to me!" shouted the owl, whose talons had been tied to a bunch of smelly garlic.

"Someone tied up my body!" complained the viper, whose whole body had been wrapped up on itself.

"My ears are all clogged with moss! I can't hear anything anymore!" said the angry fox.

The fairy Olga ran her fingers through her hair, confused, but then managed to control herself and announced: "Calm down now, my friends! I am well aware that someone here is being much too sly. This can't go on. It ends today!"

Then, she climbed on top of a big rock so that everyone could see her well. "Listen well, this is what we will do. Tonight, no one will sleep, not even for a minute! If we all do this, we have a good chance of figuring out who is responsible for the pranks, by catching them in the act! Whoever finds the culprit just has to call my name and then I'll take care of them!"

Thus, night fell, and all the animals pretended to go to sleep as usual, but they were actually alert, awake, and ready to act.

At some point, while the wolf was sitting in his den, he heard some strange noises, and then two small voices, "Psss.... Quick, quick!" whispered one small voice.

"Ha ha ha ha, tomorrow morning we will have a good laugh at the wolf!" replied the other small voice.

They didn't have time to do anything, because suddenly they were caught by the wolf, who held them tightly within his paws. "Give me a good reason not to eat you, mischievous elves!"

They were "Duru" and "Kai," two young elves from the village of the leaf. The two looked at each other with very worried expressions and tried to beg for mercy.

"I know what I'll do with you!" exclaimed the laughing wolf, and then he called the name of the fairy Olga so loudly that all the animals heard him.

In no time, they had all arrived there to finally find out who was responsible for all those stupid pranks. When the fairy arrived, the animals were in complete silence.

"Duru and Kai of the village of the leaf!" announced the fairy. Then, she looked at them with a strange smile and went on saying, "Well well, I see that while the other elves make themselves useful in all the forest, you two only carry out pranks, hurting everyone!"

Duru and Kai tried to open their mouths to make an excuse, but they were transformed into bushes by the fairy Olga before they could do that.

"You will remain like this for a whole month! Without even being able to move! This way, you will have the opportunity to reflect on your actions and on the suffering that you caused to the others!" This made all the animals burst out laughing.

From that day on, for a month, whoever walked by those bushes always had a big laugh. When Duru and Kai went back to normal, they never dared to do these kinds of pranks again. It seemed that they had learned their lesson, since they became very helpful towards everyone.

**MORAL:** A small prank won't hurt anyone, and it can be amusing. However, when the prank is too annoying, there's a chance it could hurt someone. Before you do something like that, it's important to ask yourself whether you'd want someone else to do it to you. If the answer is "no," then you shouldn't do it to someone else.

## The Elephant Who Didn't Know he was Strong

A long time ago, in a remote village in the middle of a green jungle, there lived an elephant called Bombo. He had been named by his owners who had raised him ever since he was a baby. Now, however, he had grown so much that he towered over the small stone houses in front of the marketplace where he had lived for all his life.

Bombo had never left that place except for his weekly baths in the lake of the nearby oasis right behind the marketplace.

You might be asking yourselves why Bombo never left that village square.

That's because his rear leg was bound by a small chain. That's right, Bombo was chained to a well and his owners didn't free him. Even though they loved the elephant dearly, they were too afraid that he might run away and never come back.

"I would really, really like to know what there is out there other than the village, inside the jungle" said Bombo, snorting. "Maybe there are other animals like me there in the jungle. Will it be dangerous? What if I see a mouse?" He was really scared of mice, but he also really wanted to see the world, and so he spent his days imagining what there could be outside the village.

Every day was the same in the marketplace: eat, sleep, then eat, sleep, eat again, sleep, and bath-time.

All the people of the village loved Bombo, especially the children who often brought him some peanuts as a gift. As more time passed, Bombo grew strangely melancholic, and he always dreamed of the same thing, the green jungle.

Even the humans had noticed that Bombo was becoming sadder as time went by, but they often told each other: "He has a place to sleep, he has as much food as he wants, and he has everything in life. What else could he possibly need?"

Bombo didn't know that soon something would change his life forever.

On a day like any other, he heard a little voice whispering from behind the well. "Psss, hey you!" Bombo whirled around, but he couldn't understand what was making that noise. He didn't see anything there!

Once more, the little voice spoke, "Hey there, giant! Throw me that peanut near your legs!"

Bombo immediately exclaimed, "Who's talking to me?"

The little voice replied, "Quick! Before that horrible striped cat comes! Not everyone is as big as you, you know!"

"Are you my conscience?" asked Bombo. "How else could you be inside my head?"

"I'm definitely not your conscience! Neither do I live in your head for that matter!" said the strange voice. "Look carefully, I'm here behind the well! I'm small but hungry, and now do throw me that peanut quickly!".

As soon as Bombo realized that the strange voice was actually a little mouse, he did what any elephant tied to a well would have done in his place. He fainted on the spot without even saying "ah."

When Bombo woke up, the little voice resumed talking to him: "Hey giant! My name is Squit, and I come from the green jungle! Please throw me a peanut, and I'll help you take that chain off!" Bombo fainted again, whispering: "I really can't stand mice!"

When Bombo regained consciousness, he jumped back up on his feet and shouted. "Did you say 'green jungle' or did I dream that?"

"I said just that because that's where I come from. Please stay calm: I'm very hungry, but I'm not a bad mouse!" Squit explained calmly.

"What do you know of the green forest, little one?" said Bombo bravely, trying to gather his courage after the big fright.

So, Squit jumped out of the well and said, "Gosh! I've never seen an elephant who was scared of a small mouse like me before in the green jungle!" The mouse burst out laughing. "Us mice eat cheese and peanuts, and we definitely don't eat gray giants like you! How can a big beast like you possibly be kept bound to such a small chain? This sure is funny!"

"You only talk this way because you've never been chained to a well before" said Bombo, who was slowly gaining courage and becoming more familiar with the tiny animal. After all, if the mouse had wanted to hurt Bombo, he would've already done so, right? This was his first time talking to a mouse, and he was starting to think that they weren't as dangerous as he had always believed.

"If I give you my peanuts, could you break this chain for me?" Bombo asked with a stutter.

"Of course not! You'll be the one to break it!" Squit replied with confidence and was happily looking at the shower of peanuts coming from Bombo's trunk. A new friendship had just been born. On that day, something different from the usual had happened, something that had never happened before.

"I tried to break this chain countless times!" sighed Bombo sadly. "When I was small it was the only thing I thought about, but I was never strong enough to do it. Why would today be any different?" he concluded, looking at his leg.

So Squit, laughing loudly, exclaimed, "It's simple, you're not so small now. Now, you're bigger than anyone else in this village. That's why you'll be able to do it! Give it a good pull and show me how strong you a-" Squit couldn't even finish his sentence when a dull noise echoed throughout the market. Bombo had broken the chain with one firm movement, and a piece of the wall had come off from the well! Everyone, really everyone, was shocked by what had happened.

"Whaaaaaaaat?" shouted Bombo suddenly. "For all the peanuts in the village! I'm free! I was tied to this well for all this time because I didn't think I could ever break free!" He then started dancing through all of the marketplace as if he was crazy.

"How can I ever thank you for your help, Squit?" asked Bombo.

"Help me return to the forest! There aren't any evil cats there," replied Squit. "We could go to the green jungle together if you let me travel on your back! I weigh as much as a bag of peanuts and you won't even feel that I'm there, I promise!"

So, the two friends left the village, and no one dared stop them. Neither the villagers nor the cats, who watched in disbelief, even tried to stop them as a mouse passed by, waving at them from the back of an elephant.

From that day onwards, Bombo was able to visit the green jungle and to live with all the other elephants of his species. He never forgot the place where he was born and raised, and so he often came back to see his owners and the children of the village. The humans, seeing him come back to them, realized that there had never been a need to keep him chained, since a real bond isn't made of chains, but of willingness to be together. Bombo used the freedom he had gained to return to what had previously been his prison of his own free will.

When Bombo returned to the green jungle, he now had a family waiting for him and a small peanut-eating friend.

**MORAL:** People need to be allowed to be themselves. Only then will they find the strength to become who they have always dreamed of being. People decide to stay together because they care for each other and not because they're forced to do so.

# Mission Earth: A Story of Aliens

Once upon a time, there were three alien heroes on a special mission. They came from a galaxy far away and they traveled on a spaceship that looked like a bubble. Their planet was dying, and the only solution was to perform a heroic deed. This mission was to explore the universe, looking for a new home and a new planet for the alien "Bumbu" race.

Unfortunately, the pilots weren't very skillful, so they were forced to make an emergency landing on the closest planet, Earth.

Pop and Toc, the pilots, immediately realized what mess they had ended up in while B2, the robot who accompanied them, was already calculating what dangers they would have to face: "Master, I would like to remind you that this planet is inhabited by a very dangerous species called "humans" and the probabili-"

B2 was quickly interrupted by Pop who shouted, "Will you be quiet you piece of junk? You've constantly been talking about this Earth for five galaxies, and now because you couldn't stop talking about Earth, we ended up landing right on top of it! You brought us bad luck!"

"But...but, Master..." said B2. "No buts!" replied Pop, who was frustrated because of what had happened. "If instead of spending all your time oiling your gears, you had instead paid attention to the route, we wouldn't have run out of blue energy!" continued Pop undeterred.

Toc, who was the calmest of the three, cut in, "Relax, calm down you two, we don't have much time left before someone sees us, which would cause us some trouble. We need to repair the ship as quickly as we can!"

Having said that, the three heroes started looking for blue energy to refuel their spaceship, but they quickly realized that there was nothing but rocks and desert around them.

In the meantime, in a farm near the landing site, a boy called Jack, sitting in his room, had seen a strange white light that looked like a bubble of energy fall from the sky. The light had fallen right inside the valley. "I absolutely must find out what that light was!" said Jack, while hurriedly jumping onto his bike and racing towards the strange light.

Meanwhile, B2, who was following the pilots as best as he could, suddenly stopped and tried to say, "Master, if we keep going in this direction, it's likely that we will find some human beings. I've heard that they eat mechanical parts like mine... yes sir, and I've also read that-"

"B2, let's try to focus on the mission" cut in Toc, who was desperately looking for any traces of blue energy by pointing a strange flashing device towards the sky.

"But master..." continued B2, "let me remind you of the law number 28, chapter 4, that says: Never ever ever ever go near planet Earth or the humans. The probabili-"

He couldn't even finish his sentence, when Pop threw Toc's water bottle at him and shouted angrily, "this robot must have drunk too much oil during the journey. I've always said that we shouldn't let him have too much oil! Can't you see that he ends up not listening to our orders, Toc?"

Toc replied worriedly, "Rather, I think that we're going too far from the spaceship. Maybe we should've left B2 inside to keep watch. We better go back to the spaceship for today. We'll just end up getting lost if we keep walking in random directions."

So, the three desperate heroes changed direction to go back to the base and come up with a better plan. Meanwhile Jack, who had arrived at the source of the light, couldn't believe what he was seeing. "An alien spaceship? A real spaceship? It's my lucky day!" shouted Jack, who couldn't restrain himself. So, he recklessly entered the ship, intending to play inside of it. Indeed, he thought that this was a great opportunity.

Mary and Paul, who had returned to the farm, couldn't find their son Jack and, becoming very worried, started shouting his name all over the farm. "Jaaaaack! Where are you? Jaaaack! Mom and dad are looking for you!" They couldn't find Jack anywhere. It was as if he had vanished into thin air.

Meanwhile, as they were returning to the spaceship, Pop, Toc, and B2 were thoughtful. They couldn't stay on Earth for long, since the survival of the Bumbu depended entirely on their mission.

"There are millions of galaxies, and we just had to end up on the most dangerous planet that there is," repeated B2.

"Now I'll turn off that pile of junk of a robot!" snorted Pop, while he opened the spaceship's hatch. However, as soon as they got inside their ship, they realized that something was off. It was as if someone had been inside while they were gone and had left a great mess. Jack had played inside the ship until he passed out on some kind of bed, exhausted.

"Master! Our ship is contaminated! A human!" shouted B2 as loudly as he could, while running madly around the spaceship and crashing into the walls. The three aliens, astounded, found Jack on the bed, who woke up with a start, shouting out of fear.

Pop, who was the most impulsive one, shouted without thinking, "get out of our ship right now, you disgusting creature, go! Shoo!"

"Can't you see that he's scared?" said Toc, who was trying to make the strange creature who was now awake and panicking, calm down. "This must be a human cub, look at how small and helpless he is. If he had wanted to hurt us, he would've already done so. We should bring him with us!".

B2 quickly cut in. "Master, let me remind you that, according to the galactic manual, human beings can eat all kinds of things, and they can even eat five Bumbu all at once!" Pop and Toc were too eager to learn about this alien life form to listen to B2's complaints, and so they tried to communicate with the human cub who didn't seem to be scared of them anymore, and in fact found everything rather funny, almost as if it was all a game.

"I can't come with you. I have a family here on Earth," explained Jack. "Family? What's a family?" asked the curious Toc.

Jack replied, "a family is when people live together and love each other very much, even if they sometimes argue with each other." He didn't have the time to start a new sentence when the roar of a car arriving at great speed was heard outside. It was Paul and Mary who had followed the bicycle's tracks all the way to the spaceship.

"Mom! Dad!" shouted Jack, who ran towards them to give them a hug.

"Here you go, master!" said B2, "we're surrounded. More humans have arrived! When humans squeeze each other like that, it means that they're getting ready to go to war! Those two humans are much bigger than the cub!" continued B2 with a scared tone.

"Can you drop the galactic manual for once? Can't you see that those two just came looking for their child? Maybe they can help us!" said Pop with hope.

Even though Mary and Paul were at first terrified, Jack quickly explained that there was nothing to be afraid of except for maybe the robot, that talking piece of junk who had probably lost some gears. Pop and Toc explained their situation to the parents, who patiently listened to the whole story.

"How does this blue energy that you need in order to continue your travels look?" asked Paul inquisitively. Toc returned with a jar between his hands: "Here, this is our fuel! We're lost without it!"

Mary gasped, "But that's just plain old water! Is your spaceship powered by water? What a marvelous technology!"

"Water? Is that what you humans call blue energy?" replied Pop immediately.

Toc, Pop and B2 were brought to the farm, where they were allowed to take all the water they needed to travel for at least another twelve galaxies, there and back! Even B2, who so far had been very distrustful, had happily started to describe their planet and its laws to the humans. They were ready to resume their journey.

"Dear friends, may you have a good journey, and I hope that you will find what you're looking for!" said Paul, waving to the three travelers.

"What is a friend?" asked B2. Jack replied right away: "A friend is when you care about someone, even if you don't live with them, and you like to help them and to know that they're doing well without getting anything in exchange." Then Mary added, "Hey B2, could you do me a favor? When you return to your planet, find that galactic manual, and where it says that humans are dangerous, replace that with 'friends forever'."

"Friends forever, it will be done, thank you" waved the three aliens, and they dashed away into outer space.

**MORAL:** Not trusting strangers is fine, but you need to know a person well before deciding how to behave with them. It's better to say nothing rather than to say something rude about someone else.

# The emperor's heir

The people of the village near the royal palace woke up to the voice of the emperor's servant, who gloriously proclaimed in a loud voice.

"Tomorrow evening you're all invited to the party in honor of his grace the emperor. Come celebrate the elderly emperor, who is now old and sick, and wants to give you all a special surprise. Bring all of your possessions to the palace in order to respectfully say goodbye to the great emperor who will soon pass away."

When the servant had finished repeating the message over and over again, he closed the papyrus that contained the message and returned to the royal palace.

A great deal of bickering was then heard in the village square.

"Bring him all of our possessions? Is he crazy?"

"I only have my mule, and without it I could never farm the land!"

"I will bring him what I can if it helps the emperor in heaven. After all, he was always kind to us."

"I won't bring that stingy emperor anything because he is already full of gold!"

So, on the next day, a long line formed from the village to the palace. All the villagers were going to the party and bringing all they could. There were some people with huge carriages full of junk and others with small bags. Some were mocked because they were bringing too many things, others because they weren't bringing enough.

So, after a splendid feast full of delicacies, wine, and luxurious food came the time to say goodbye to the emperor. He was sitting on his throne of gold, inviting all of the people, one by one, to have an audience with him. One by one, they went to pay homage to him with greetings and praises.

Then came the turn of Samai, a boy with very poor parents, who came empty-handed: He was followed by the laughter of the people of the village who already expected that he would disappoint the emperor.

However, Samai said very shyly, "I couldn't bring anything, my lord, because I don't own anything. My family is very poor, but please give me the honor of helping you in your last days of life. I will give you my presence and my services. After all, you're now an old man who needs companionship and love instead of precious goods."

At that point, the emperor, looking satisfied, returned to his chambers without saying anything. All the guests were a bit disappointed because they thought that he had forgotten about the surprise. When they were all getting ready to leave, the faithful servant made another announcement.

"The emperor thanks you and wants you to know that all of those who brought something will be compensated with the weight of their present in gold. So, whoever brought more will also receive more. The young Samai, who brought everything he had, which is himself and his precious time, will be given the greatest reward!"

"You should all know that the emperor doesn't have any relatives, and he has been looking for a special heir for quite some time. There is no better person to give everything to, than someone who is willing to give everything he has."

Everyone gasped and some people complained while others clapped.

So, they all left the palace, some happy and full of gold while others were empty-handed, angry, and frustrated.

Samai, however, finally had a safe place where he could live with his parents for all his life. The empire had a new ruler who was caring and kind-hearted.

**MORAL:** It's important to give even when we don't have much. We shouldn't give in order to receive something in exchange, but because we enjoy doing so. One day, we might even be rewarded for this.

# The Unicorn Without a Horn

A legend says that if you follow a rainbow, you may find precious treasure where it ends. Every respectable rainbow is born after a good storm when the sun returns.

Margot was a little girl who loved dreaming about unicorns, some of the most famous magical animals in the kingdom of imagination. Right after it rained, she would always wait for the rainbow to arrive because she knew that the best way to find a unicorn is to look carefully above a rainbow.

"Margot, don't stay near the window all day, and come help me" was a phrase often repeated by her father.

He was a fairly strict man, and his life had been very hard ever since his wife passed away, but he was very worried about Margot because he didn't want her to end up like him. That's why he decided that Margot would have to study and become as educated as possible.

"Are you still looking for those unicorns? I've already told you that they went extinct a long time ago. I've seen all kinds of things in my life. I've seen monsters with four arms, I've met fairies, famous sorcerers, and even some elves, but I have never seen a unicorn in all of my life!" explained her father patiently.

Things weren't going so well. It hadn't rained for many seasons and the harvest was a disaster. The surroundings had become so dry that practically no vegetation grew anymore. Abacus, Margot's father, was one of the many farmers who had been hurt by the great drought. His harvest decreased day by day and he barely managed to feed himself and his daughter.

Margot had the same dream every night about a white horse on top of a hill. "Daddy! It was him again! I saw him again!" she would shout loudly.

"For now, we'll focus on your education, and then you'll come to help me in the fields, and no buts!" snorted her father, who was tired of hearing the same story about unicorns. This had been going on for years.

The following day, Abacus went to the village to sell the few tomatoes he had been able to harvest. He noticed a big tent that he had never seen before, and its sign, decorated by a rainbow with seven colors, read: "I predict the future here, but don't ask me about the past." Since all kinds of magical creatures passed through the village to rest there or to earn some bread, Abacus was attracted by the rainbow above the sign and looked in his pocket to see how much money he had. He sighed, and then went inside.

"So, what would you like to know about your future?" asked an old lady who was wearing a hood inside the tent. She had a deck of cards next to an almost completely worn candle, and she gestured at Abacus with her hands to take a seat. "You already know why you're here, right?" Asked the fortune teller with a smirk.

"I want to know what will happen to my family and my work, to our village, and whether the water will come back" replied Abacus.

"Oh no!" replied abruptly the old lady, and she continued: "You came here because you're looking for the rainbow. That's the real reason!"

Abacus curled up his nose and, unconvinced, said, "What does a rainbow have to do with anything? I really don't understand!"

The fortune teller, without even bothering to reply, started to move all her cards and arranged them on the table, whispering, "Mhh...mh...mh" and then, "Now, I understand everything."

"I don't understand anything!" Abacus impatiently replied, already wanting to leave that tent.

The fortune teller explained that if Abacus wanted to see rain again, he would have to look for the rainbow in the only place where it could be hiding. "Rainbows are a bridge between reality and magic. I can't help you, but there is someone else who can!" Then, she gathered up all of the cards again and started to change the candle.

"What you said doesn't make any sense! Everyone knows that there can't be rainbows without rain. Now you're telling me to find a rainbow in order to get some rain?" shouted Abacus furiously.

"That's what the cards say! Don't get angry at me! I'm just a poor fortune teller!" the old lady shouted back.

Then Abacus, who was a bit disappointed, got up and went away, muttering to himself. "What a horrible old woman! I should've kept my money instead of wasting it like that!"

"Who are you calling horrible old woman? I heard that, you ungrateful man!" shouted the fortune teller from far away, but by now, Abacus was too far to hear her.

A few days went by, and the ground became drier and drier, but there didn't seem to be any solution. All of the village was in a crisis, and soon they would all be in danger if things continued this way. One night, Margot woke up with a start, shouting, and darted into her father's bed.

"The unicorn was there on the hill! He wasn't well!" cried Margot with a shaky voice.

"It's just the same dream as usual, now try to get some sleep, because tomorrow will be a long day!" said Abacus while he stroked her hair.

"This time it was different" explained Margot, "the unicorn needed help and he was lit by a great rainbow in the sky. He was asking me to find the oldest oak tree."

All of a sudden, Abacus jumped on his feet and started walking all around the room, deep in thought. He then abruptly said, "You said that the unicorn of your dreams is on top of a hill, right? The oldest oak tree of the area is on top of the hill at the foot of the mountains. Maybe, this is what that horrible old woman was talking about!"

Hence, in the morning the two set out towards the hill. Abacus remembered that he had always used to play near the old oak tree when he was a little boy. It used to be the fairies' house a long time ago, but no one had lived in there for years. Once they reached the top of the hill, they couldn't believe their eyes. A beautiful white horse was caught by a hunter's trap. He was by now resigned to death and was lying on the ground below the oak tree.

"The unicorn! The unicorn, it's here!" shouted Margot, jumping all over the place.

"Don't be silly, it's just an injured horse!" replied Abacus, who was meanwhile forcing the trap open with a stick. Then, the trap gave a thud, it finally opened, and the horse was free.

At the same time, the head of the horse started giving off a very bright light, and a golden horn grew out of his forehead. His tail was dyed with the seven colors of the rainbow. They couldn't believe their eyes. They had really found a unicorn!

"Thanks to you, I'm back to being myself!" exclaimed the unicorn. "Some hunters trapped me and took away my horn, and with it my magic. For months, I was stuck here without being able to call for help except for in the dreams of children. Now, thanks to you, I can finally fly again! You two should follow the rainbow, and you will find what you're looking for!"

Having said that, the unicorn flew away and a heavy rain started falling, for the first time in months, and people started singing and shouting out of joy.

When they arrived at the village, Abacus and Margot noticed that it had stopped raining and that a huge rainbow had formed in the valley. So, the two ran towards the end of the rainbow. Surprisingly, they discovered that the valley was full of sprouting seeds and small plants. They had found the treasure at the end of the rainbow, the valley had become green again!

**MORAL:** When things aren't going well, a surprise could be waiting for us just around the corner. Things can always improve if we believe in it.

## Wanting Too Much

A long, long time ago, on a small island of warriors, there lived a boy called Sanui,, together with his grandpa. The young Sanui was found on the seashore when he was still a baby, lying on a rolled-up rope inside a boat that seemed abandoned. Maui wasn't Sanui's real grandpa, but when he found the baby, he decided to raise him as his grandson and never to tell him about the truth.

Everyone on the island was strong and brave including the women. It was how life on the island was. You were either strong, or you had to become strong. So, Maui tried to raise Sanui into one of the island's strongest warriors, the greatest honor you could have there.

Sanui, who was frail and clumsy, could never keep up with his grandpa's expectations and always ended up disappointing him in one way or another. No matter how hard he tried, he was never good enough for his grandpa.

So Sanui grew up wishing to be accepted by Maui, and he would've done anything in order to become as strong as his grandpa wanted. Except that Sanui had his own way of showing that he was strong.

"I will travel the seven seas, and when I come back with treasure from all over the world, then my grandpa will acknowledge my strength!" said Sanui while building a boat. Sadly, however, he never managed to go further than the fishermen's island, which was only fifty kilometers away.

Despite this, he never gave up, and he always came up with new plans to prove his strength. "I will build some wings for myself and I'll fly to the moon with those, and when I return, everyone will have to admit that I'm strong!" Sanui actually managed to fly that day, but he could never go higher than the top of the island's volcano.

Even though many people made fun of him, Sanui never gave up and continued to do these challenges undeterred. "I will figure out how to fish a whale, and the island will have enough food for months, and I will become the hero of the village!" But this time, he ended up catching many small fish, and not one gigantic whale.

Until the day came when Sanui had to admit that he wasn't as good as the others. His constant failures had demoralized him. "Grandpa Maui, forgive me for not being able to become the man you have always wanted me to be."

His grandpa, who had recently been observing Sanui very carefully, didn't say anything, and instead gathered all of the villagers on the beach and started giving a speech.

"Ladies and gentlemen, today I learned that being different isn't necessarily a bad thing. Today, I realized that the worth of a person doesn't only depend on one type of achievement, as Sanui has taught to all of us." he admitted reluctantly.

"Sanui wanted to catch a whale for everyone, and while it's true that he couldn't do it, he still managed to catch many small fish, thanks to his intelligence. He caught more fish than anyone on this island had been able to before. Thanks to him, we'll have plenty to eat for weeks!" continued Maui, while everyone listened in silence.

"Sanui wanted to reach the moon, but even though he didn't manage to do that, he still found a way to build wings that let him fly. Thanks to that, we'll be able to see the sea currents from above and travel more safely." The faces of the warriors were starting to change.

"Sanui wanted to travel the seven seas, but he only managed to reach the nearby fishermen's island. Thanks to him, we'll be able to see our distant family members on that island again. Let me remind you that no one has been able to reach that island in years because of the dangerous currents!"

The warriors were starting to see the skinny and weak boy in a new light.

Maui continued, "Sanui has shown us that if we aim very high, beyond our limits, we can achieve incredible goals. I, for one, didn't have any faith in him, because I expected him to grow up like everyone else."

Sanui's eyes were starting to fill with hope, and all his failures were starting to weigh less on him. He started to see them as achievements instead.

"Sanui," concluded Grandpa Maui, "I want you to know that I'm proud of you, and I'm happy to have you in my life and I don't care about what you accomplish anymore. I will always love you, and I'm sorry for having been so blind!"

Sanui started crying out of happiness, while everyone proclaimed him the first and only inventor of the island of warriors.

**MORAL:** In this world, we're all different from each other. You shouldn't try to become like everyone else. You should instead be yourself while respecting other people's differences.

# The Farm where the Animals Didn't Understand Each Other

Once upon a time, there was a farm in the countryside with many animals. However, ever since the dog, Rosco, had passed away, there wasn't anyone on the farm who could talk to everyone. It is well known that dogs are very good at understanding both humans and animals. That's why Rosco was excellent at running the farm, especially since the farmer couldn't make himself understood using human language.

Rosco had been gone for months and everyone missed him. In fact, the farm was a mess. No one could understand each other anymore, and the various jobs necessary to keep the farm going were not carried out.

The days were more or less always the same. "Moooo?" asked the cow. "Baaaaaa" replied the sheep. "Cluck-cluck?" chorused the hens.

Then, there were the donkey, the cat, the rooster, the rabbits, the frogs, the pigs, the goats, and many other animals. "Meow?" – "ribbit-ribbit!" – "Cock-a-doodle-doo!" – "quack-quack!?" – "squit-squit!" – "roaaar!" – "oink-oink!" Basically, it was all a huge mess. They all spoke in their own language, and the animals just ended up confusing each other. The animals could neither understand each other nor understand the farmer, and the farm was suffering from the consequences of this.

"Where is the milk today?" shouted the farmer. "This rooster broke! He didn't wake me up again this morning!" None of the animals listened to him anymore, and the situation was getting worse and worse.

So, one day, the desperate farmer brought a surprise to the farm from his van. It was Billy, a German shepherd dog with very young fur, who seemed grown-up, in good health, and also very helpful.

The enthusiastic animals immediately explained their problem to their new friend. They told him about Rosco, and how nice it was when there was someone who could communicate between the owner and them.

Recently, all the farmer did was scold them. But all they managed to make out from his shouting was: "Bla-bla-bla-bla-bla-bla-bla." They couldn't understand the human language at all.

Billy immediately understood the problem and spent some time getting to know the animals, the farmer, their needs, and the situation rapidly got better. Then, one day, the dog decided to gather all the animals to give a speech.

"Dear friends, I know that you expect me to help you understand each other, and that this way you will also be able to make the owner happy. Today, I'd like to teach you something more important than that. Today, I'd like to reveal the secret of us dogs".

The surprised animals were very interested in Billy's speech.

"Us dogs can understand all living beings. Do you know why? It's because we can listen to what is being said! You don't necessarily need to know everyone's language. You just need to understand the people around you. This is how I managed to learn the languages of all living beings!" said Billy, while all the animals listened carefully.

"Starting from today, I want you to spend some time with an animal of another species. Observe him, look at him, and try to learn his habits. Appreciate him for being part of the same farm, and look at how he moves, what he eats, until you know everything about him. Then, change partner, until you end up knowing everyone in the farm."

And he concluded, "even the owner has some needs. Try to understand what they are, and you'll see that instead of an enemy, he'll turn into a great partner. He will bring you food and he'll become your servant!"

So, all the animals quickly started to understand that they all had their own job inside the farm. They learned everyone else's preferences and habits, they started giving the farmer what he needed, and the owner started to take better care of them.

The animals had learned to understand each other, and not only through language. In the end, even the farmer started making himself more understood.

Billy had taught everyone that they couldn't just rely on others, but that they had to learn about the world with their own eyes and ears, whether they be humans or animals!

**MORAL:** Even if it can be hard to understand others, we can improve this situation by putting ourselves in someone else's shoes. Each person has his or her own needs, and if we learn to listen to them, then it will be easier to understand that person.

# The King of the Whole World

When king Atlas was at the height of his power, he had already managed to achieve everything possible for a human being. He had the most powerful army of the whole world and every country fell to his might.

He had won every battle, defeated incredible enemies, killed dragons, captured the scariest monsters, and locked up evil witches and wizards. The name of the great king Atlas and his troops was renowned all over the world.

Despite all this, there was something wrong with the king, there was something he was missing, even though he was the most powerful man on all the continents.

"Why am I not happy? I have all the land I want, all the gold of the world, and as much food as I want. I have servants who obey me, and my warriors are always ready to carry out any of my orders" said Atlas worriedly.

He had felt this way ever since he started conquering lands. It was never enough for him, and so he became more and more greedy for power.

As time went by, and as his number of possessions grew, that strange feeling inside him kept getting stronger. Like a brick in his stomach, that feeling was always there to remind him that he didn't have enough. A voice inside his head kept saying, "I still need more. This isn't enough."

One day, the king decided that he couldn't bear all that pain anymore, so he called for three teachers from Asia who could teach him their wisdom. Thus, the first one arrived.

"Oh holy teacher, you who know people's souls, tell me, why is it that I still don't feel happy even though I own everything?"

The first teacher replied, "try asking yourself that, instead of asking a stranger for advice!"

The king wasn't at all satisfied with that answer. So, he called the second teacher.

"Oh holy teacher, you who know people's souls, tell me, why is it that I still don't feel happy even though I own everything?"

The second master replied, "You just answered your own question, my wise king."

King Atlas couldn't understand what that meant, and he was starting to lose his patience. So, he called the third one.

"Oh holy teacher, you who know people's souls, tell me, why is it that I still don't feel happy even though I own everything?"

The third teacher stared into the king's eyes and then left without saying anything.

At that point, Atlas became furious. "You're lucky that I haven't cut your heads off! You came here all the way from Asia just to tell me what I already know?" he shouted, and then he retired to his quarters.

One day, after winning a battle, having conquered the enemy's city walls, he saw a little girl and couldn't take his eyes off her. She took the last piece of bread from her small pockets and gave it to the wounded.

He was also surprised by the little girl's proud and brave smile. Even though she didn't have anything left, she was ready to do anything to help those in need, and she did this with great serenity, something that the king had never seen before.

"Teacher! Thanks to you, I finally understood what I was missing!" said the crying king Atlas, hugging the little girl.

He had spent all his life taking away everything from people. He never realized that he could instead share what he had. He didn't have anyone to protect or anyone to take care of, and it was other people who took care of him.

From that day onwards, King Atlas spent the rest of his life giving back what he had previously conquered with violence. The more he gave, the more a new emotion grew in him. For the first time, he felt happy and proud. **MORAL:** One of the best ways to feel happy about ourselves is to share our things, or our time, with other people. This can make us feel better, especially when we see their happy faces.

# The Porcupine who Couldn't Hug Anyone

A porcupine called Ricciola had built her home inside a big tree at the base of the trunk. There was a nice warm bed, a hall with a view of the forest, and lots of space for the winter supplies. In fact, it was here that Ricciola spent the long winters, warmed by the sun shining on the tree, safe from bad weather and dangerous animals.

Ricciola had always wanted to share her home with her friends because she had lived alone all her life. She barely remembered her mom, whom she had lost sight of one day near the great river, and never saw again. Unfortunately, Ricciola had never been able to find someone who wanted to live with her because there was one small problem, she really loved hugs.

She hadn't received enough affection as a child, so she had told herself that she would show her love for everyone around her as an adult. There was no better way to do that for a porcupine, than to try to hug all the animals of the forest. Sadly, the other animals didn't really appreciate this since it meant getting their bodies covered in spikes. So, they ended up avoiding her.

"Hey, friend bear! It's been such a long time! Come here and give me one of your oak-tree-breaking hugs!" said Ricciola, running towards the bear.

"Don't you try to touch me! The last time you did that I had spikes stuck in my butt for days!" replied the bear, while he climbed up a tree trying to run from the porcupine. He stayed up there until she was gone.

"Hello hare!" said Ricciola, seeing the hare jump rapidly. "I see that you're in a hurry again today! Why don't you relax a bit here with me and give me a hug?"

"Oh no, my dear porcupine, you won't trick me this time! The last time I hugged you, I couldn't leave my burrow for a whole month," replied the hare.

"I'm a hare and running is what I do! I don't hug other animals. You're a porcupine, and loving you is very, very painful. I'm a hare and you're a porcupine! Hare, porcupine, hare, porcupine...do you understand? You should try to hug the trees and not us poor animals!" Having said that, the hare disappeared over the horizon.

"Hey friend owl, come here and let me squeeze you a little!" shouted Ricciola, when she saw the animal flying near her. Before she could even finish speaking, the owl had already flown up on top of a fir tree, to safety, and looking down he shouted anxiously, "you crazy porcupine! The last time you hugged me, I was left with so many spikes on me, that not even my family could recognize me anymore! They even stopped hugging me!" The owl hid between the tree's leaves.

So, Ricciola went around the forest looking for hugs, but no one seemed to be willing to show her some affection. Besides, her own spikes didn't bother her at all. Why did everyone else care about them so much?

The animals of the forest weren't being mean, they just didn't want to get hurt. In fact, sometimes they went to see Ricciola in her home, but she always ended up asking for a hug, and the poor visitor got injured!

On other occasions, in good company, Ricciola became so emotional that her spikes were shot in every direction, and whoever was near her was in big trouble.

Tired of this situation, the animals met up to look for a solution. Ricciola was still their friend, and she wasn't a bad person, she just needed someone who could return her hugs.

"If I end up with another spike on me, I swear that I'll move to another forest this time!" said the deer.

"I care about Ricciola, but I also care about my own health" said the fox.

"I had an idea!" the bear suddenly shouted. "In the outskirts of the forest, there's someone who could maybe help us. If you listen to me, starting from tomorrow, we won't have to put up with spikes anymore!"

On the next day, they all went to Ricciola's home, bringing a guest from afar.

"Meet Spino, the animals chorused."

So, a little shyly, a hedgehog walked up to Ricciola.

"They told me that you want a hug," said the hedgehog. Then, he suddenly wrapped his arms around Ricciola, who was shocked. For the first time, she had found someone who didn't run away from her! She had understood that not all kinds of animals are made to be together. Everyone needs his or her own space.

Ricciola became so emotional, that many spikes flew off of her body in every direction. Can you guess where they went? That's right: onto the hare, the bear, the deer, the fox, and the owl, who went near her for the very last time.

**MORAL:** We can love everyone, but some people will accept our love more willingly while others will need it less. It's up to us to recognize who those people are.

# Saman and the Abandoned Dragon

Many centuries ago, there were all kinds of magical creatures, good and evil, and man had to adapt to survive as best as he could. When there was a troll around, you had to hide. When you saw a dragon, you had to run. When there was a sorcerer nearby, it was better not to anger him. Life as a human being was tough, but mankind had always managed to find a way to survive.

The young Saman lived with his family in a village at the foot of a volcano in a magical green valley, where it was always spring, and the trees never lost their leaves. One day his father, who was a merchant, brought home from a business trip something that would change their lives forever.

Saman knew well that his father, Furio, would bring him a gift from his trip as he always did, but he didn't know what kind of gift it would be. The wait was excruciating as usual.

As soon as the door opened, Saman immediately ran into his father's arms. Saman's mother, Aly, loved seeing them hug because it was the moment when the family was finally reunited.

There was a bag hanging from Furio's neck, and he took it off and gave it to Saman while saying, "this is the rarest object that I have ever found! What do you think about it?"

Saman glanced at the bag and replied, "a bag? Oh, yes, of course, thanks dad, I've always wanted this." Saman wrinkled his nose and lowered his head.

"No, silly! The present is inside the bag, try opening it!" said Furio, laughing.

Unbelievable! Inside the bag, there was a strange brown egg as big as Saman's head. "It's the egg of a dragon, and it belonged to a sorcerer who disappeared. I acquired it thanks to a friend. It could be worth a fortune someday," whispered Furio in his son's ear.

Then, he turned to Aly, who looked terrified, and he whispered to her, "Don't worry, I think that the egg is empty, and I'm not even sure that it's a dragon's. They told me that the old sorcerer was a madman!"

So, Saman went happily to his room, jumping and shouting, "I will have a dragon! I will have a dragon!"

"You won't have any dragons, young man, that egg is just a piece of furniture," replied his father, but Saman was too busy to listen.

The days went by, and although Saman prayed every night for the egg to hatch, nothing happened. More than a month had gone by without anything happening. So, sad and desperate, one day, he decided to throw the egg into the fireplace. "An empty egg is useless anyway!" he said angrily.

The moment the egg touched the embers, a crack started to form along all of its length. Saman couldn't believe his eyes. A tail came out of the egg, then two legs, then a pair of eyes. It was a small dragon! It seemed that the egg needed heat from a fire to hatch.

Aly and Furio were stunned. "What do we do now? There really was a dragon inside that egg!" they shouted in unison.

While they thought about what to do next, weeks passed, and Saman grew more attached to the dragon. He had even called him Flame, and the small creature had doubled in size in just over a month. Luckily, he couldn't breathe fire yet, but a little bit of smoke had begun to come out of his nostrils.

"We can't keep him here with us. Don't you remember what happened to our grandparents in the village?" Said the worried mother.

Furio, lowering his head, with a weak voice said, "You're right, we shouldn't mess with a dragon. Tonight, I will bring Flame down to the river and I will take his life before he can hurt us and everyone in the village. We'll just tell Saman that he ran away."

However, when Furio brought the little dragon to the river, he didn't have the courage to do anything, and so he just freed the dragon, hoping that nature would take care of him, thinking that such a small dragon wouldn't be able to survive.

Saman was shocked by the news that Flame had escaped, and those were very hard times for him. The years went by, and growing up he told himself that the dragon was just something that he had made up when he was small. He convinced himself that Flame had never existed except for in his imagination.

One day like any other, though, people started seeing black smoke coming out of the volcano, and this seemed a bit strange to everyone since the volcano wasn't active anymore. It was a beautiful sunny day in the village, and Saman had by now become a young man. He worked in the marketplace when he had the time to pay for his education.

All of a sudden, the sky was completely covered in smoke, and a monstrous scream echoed throughout the valley. Something that resembled a devil with wings appeared on top of the volcano.

"A dragon! Run away! Save yourselves!" people shouted in the marketplace.

Panic broke out in the village. A giant dragon was breathing fire on all the houses, as if on a rampage, and huge flames came out of the animal's mouth. No one remained in the village and Saman had to run away with his family. It was a disaster, and although no one had been hurt, the village had been burned to the ground. The dragon flew away, laughing and looking satisfied.

Saman had heard of dragons, but he had never seen one in all his life, or at least, so he thought. They were truly monstrous and evil creatures, but he couldn't understand why he had always thought of them as pets.

A ruckus broke out in the village. "Darn dragon! He burned down everything I owned!"

"Don't come here ever again, you fire monster!"

"We'll rebuild our village, just to spite you!"

So, in just a few weeks, the village was rebuilt, thanks to everyone's effort. Peace came back to the village. As soon as everything went back to normal, then that fiery monster appeared again. The flames once again burned down the village, and the desperate people were once again left with nothing. The dragon laughed from a distance while he flew away.

Furio, with a very worried face, confessed something to his wife Aly, "I have to tell you something, but it won't make you happy. Do you promise to stay calm?"

"I promise," said Aly.

"That day, with Flame, well I...oh I'll admit it, I couldn't do it! I just freed him in nature! I didn't think that he could possibly survive, you see?" continued Furio.

"Are you telling me that that scary monster is actually Flame?" asked his wife angrily, throwing at him everything she could get her hands on, even though she had promised to stay calm.

They didn't realize that Saman had actually heard everything they were saying, and suddenly all of his memories started flooding back like an explosion: The egg present, the fireplace, Flame, that amazing summer spent with his friend, and then the sudden disappearance.

"So, I didn't imagine it!" Shouted Saman. "All this time, you made me think that Flame never existed. How could you?"

But his parents said, "you definitely couldn't keep a dragon as a pet! Didn't you see how dangerous and fierce he became? What else could we have done?"

The village was rebuilt once more, but Saman couldn't stop thinking about Flame and about what had happened. Of course, once all the houses had been fixed again, monstrous screams came out of the volcano, as well as smoke, fire, and all the other things that dragons do. Flame was back, and he was ready to burn down everything again.

Saman disappeared while they were all running away. He had stayed behind in the village to wait for the dragon. Like a madman, he started to shout the dragon's name as loudly as he could. This time, the dragon didn't breathe fire, but instead landed next to Saman and started to smell him.

"How do you know my name?" asked the dragon.

"I gave it to you when you were small! You have no idea how much I've missed you!"

When the people of the village went to look for Saman, they couldn't believe their eyes. The village was still there and the dragon was sitting next to the young man. The dragon seemed to have found peace and the two old friends had finally met again!

"He was desperately looking for me," said Saman. "Flame never forgot about me. That's why he was burning down the houses. He thought I was in danger, trapped inside the village."

The villagers were happy that they didn't have to rebuild everything again, and they also created a personal space for Flame where he could live. From that day onwards, Saman and Flame became best friends.

**MORAL:** If you decide to adopt an animal, you must always take care of your pet because it will become a part of your family. If you really can't keep it in your home, then you must find a warm and hospitable house for it.

# Kimb Wanted to Help Everyone Grow

There was once a magical forest, known as the "middle forest". Here, there lived all kinds of creatures, but the forest was especially famous for its fairies, magical creatures so small that they could fit in the palm of your hand. Even though they were small, they weren't defenseless. Each one of them had some extraordinary abilities that I can only describe with one word, magic.

If something was wrong with the forest, it was the fairies who brought back balance. If an animal disappeared, they would find it. If a plant was sick, they would heal it. They were essentially the guardians of the forest, but this definitely didn't give them the right to do whatever they wanted.

This is because nature has some laws that must be obeyed, and if we don't respect these laws, someone will pay dearly for it. This is why mortals were given the freedom to choose so that they could make mistakes.

In the village of Great Tree, the biggest community of fairies, there was always a great bustle, day and night, night and day. Great Tree was a five-thousand-years-old oak tree, and it was born before all the other trees of the forest. For this reason, it wasn't just a normal tree, but it kept the story of all living beings. All the animals of the forest came to Great Tree for various reasons.

There was, for example, the owl, who once came to remove some spikes. "There's a crazy porcupine who wants to hug everyone! Look at what she did to me! Sometimes, love can be very very painful. Please remove these spikes from my body!" said the owl.

There was also the worker bear who complained, "Today, those bears occupied the waterfall again. They take advantage of us because we are smaller! You need to do something!"

There were then the frogs, who came to thank and to pay homage to the fairies. "Dear fairies, what would the forest be without you? Take these sweet berries as a gift in exchange for the help that you gave us with the lake!"

Such were the days in Great Tree, which had always been the heart of the whole valley, a safe haven, and the symbol of the bond between all living beings.

The fairies knew this well, which is why they treasured their magic, and they always tried to improve themselves so that they could always give a great service to whoever needed it.

Well... there's always an exception, though. Kimb, was the youngest and most inexperienced of all the fairies, she was only two hundred years old, and compared to the others, who were much much older, she still had a long way to go.

Kimb was one of those fairies who didn't wait for those in need to come to her to Great Tree, not at all! Kimb went looking for animals to help on her own.

She had been warned many times to not play God and to let other living beings decide on their own whether they needed help, but Kimb never listened. So, one day when she felt in a particularly good mood, she decided to go to the eastern part of the valley to look for glory, when she suddenly saw a strange cocoon attached to a leaf. It was certainly a caterpillar, and it seemed to want to get out of the cocoon, judging by how hard it was struggling.

"This caterpillar is choking! I will help you get out of that cocoon, mister caterpillar!" shouted Kimb with good intentions. She concentrated, a white light appeared around the cocoon, and a beautiful butterfly came out of it. Unfortunately, though, the butterfly couldn't quite manage to fly. It was as if something had gone wrong. "Put me back inside! I told you to put me back inside, you darn fairy!" shouted the butterfly with a desperate voice.

Kimb decided to bring the butterfly back with her to Great Tree. She was sure that someone there would have a solution.

Continuing his walk along a river, Kimb met a wolf's cub who was all alone. "My mom was taken away from here by a hunter, and now I'm all alone" cried the cub.

"I will bring you with me and I will take care of you until you're all grown up when you'll be able to live on your own" said Kimb proudly, and they went on with their walk.

When they arrived near a big rock behind a waterfall, Kimb saw a lizard who had lost her tail while trying to climb up the rock. "Poor little lizard! You're lucky that I'm here to heal you" said Kimb. She started to concentrate and a white light appeared on the lizard's tail which magically reattached itself to the lizard's body.

The lizard didn't seem to be well, and in fact she started to cry even harder than before. So, Kimb took the lizard with her and dejectedly decided to return home because her magic didn't seem to be working very well.

Once she was back in Great Tree, Kimb asked the elderly fairy for advice to understand what went wrong. Even though she had done everything she could to help those animals, it simply hadn't worked.

So, the old fairy, having listened to Kimb's story, sighed and said, "dear Kimb, today you demonstrated that you have good intentions for all the animals of the forest, but sadly there are still many things that you don't understand."

Then, she removed the tail from the lizard, put the butterfly back in the cocoon, and freed the wolf cub.

"What are you doing, elderly fairy? All my work is now for nothing!" exclaimed Kimb, who was a bit surprised.

So, the old fairy spoke again: "You see, Kimb, the butterfly couldn't fly because she didn't have enough strength, and she can only get that when she is still a caterpillar. The caterpillar needs to find his own way, otherwise he never will once he gets out of the cocoon."

Then, she stroked the cub's fur and added, "You can't keep this cub as your pet and then make him live alone once grown up, because if he doesn't learn to hunt from a young age, in the future he will not know how to get by on his own."

Then, as she freed the lizard, she said, "Lizards sometimes lose their tail, but this isn't a bad thing because it just grows back on its own! If you reattach the old tail, the new one won't be able to come out and the lizard will feel pain."

Then, she stroked Kimb's head and concluded with: "There are things that not even us fairies can do with magic. Sometimes, you just have to let nature take its course. There's no other way, do you understand now?"

Kimb nodded happily. She had learned many things today and she had understood that she could help many animals, but that first she would have to study the laws of nature more!

**MORAL:** Plants, animals and even human beings, all have their own cycle of life. You don't have to force this cycle. Sometimes it's better to be patient and let nature act on its own.

# Dora and the Messages to the Universe

In Dora's family, there was a particular habit that her mother had taught her from an early age. Once a month, Dora had to write down some messages and send them to the universe. This habit had been passed down in their family for generations. Write down on a piece of paper a wish that you want to ask to the universe. Dora then had to leave the piece of paper somewhere in the house, in the garden, or in school to ensure that this wish would one day come true. Lastly, she had to give thanks in advance and wait patiently.

In fact, the house was full of pieces of paper with wishes in them which were hidden everywhere. They were under furniture, inside pots and pans, in the bathroom, in the garage, and even inside the pillow covers. Dora's mom loved to secretly read these wishes, and when she could, she tried to make sure that they came true. Sometimes she didn't even have to do anything because some things simply came true on their own.

When Dora was very small, her mom found wishes like these.

"I would really like a new doll."

"I wish that no one pulled my hair anymore in school."

"I wish that the monster under the bed became my friend."

"I would like to have twelve cats, a monkey, and if possible, even a hippo."

When Dora had grown up a little, her wishes would read as follows.

"I would like to have a boyfriend who loves me."

"I wish I had a scooter."

"I would really like to find a job."

Although Dora was growing up, she never lost the habit of writing down what she wanted the most. This helped her understand what it was that she wanted from life. It also helped her understand what she didn't want.

However, by the time Dora became a mom many years later, she had almost entirely given up on this habit, which by now she only carried out once a year, on New Year's Day. The reason for this was that, as the years went by, she had realized that these wishes didn't always come true, and often nothing at all happened.

She wasn't sure whether she wanted to continue her family's tradition because she didn't want her own daughter to also be disappointed by wishes that didn't come true.

One day, she decided to go visit her elderly mother in the house where she had grown up to find out why her family had this strange tradition.

"You see, mom, you have no idea how much I wanted to get that new job, or a new car, or to always be healthy, and who knows how many other wishes, but life didn't always seem to go like I wanted. Why did you teach me to do something like that?" asked Dora.

Her mom, smiling, went to the closet and came back with a big cardboard box. Inside it were many wishes written by Dora when she was a little girl. Her mom had kept them all her life with lots of love.

They spent hours and hours reading all the wishes again, crying and laughing, reminiscing about the past, and noticing how the wishes had changed as Dora grew up.

"Dear Dora, I knew that you would ask me this question one day," said her mother sweetly. Then, while pouring a cup of tea, she started to explain. "Did you notice how your wishes changed over the years? We often think that we want something, but are we ever really sure that it's the right thing for us?"

"When we want something, we then have to work hard to actually obtain it, and this is the beauty of life. We don't know what will happen in the future, but we can try our hardest to ensure that our wishes come true."

Then, she patiently went on, "Tough times exist so that we can get stronger. We face danger in order to become braver. We help other people in order to discover what love is."

Dora was starting to understand what her mom was trying to say.

Then her mom concluded with this. "If something doesn't go how we want, then we fall down, get back on our feet, and try again, and again, and again, until we manage to succeed."

Dora realized that she had always hoped that the universe would make her wishes come true, when it was actually her own job. She hadn't been given what she wanted, but instead what she needed in order to make her own wishes come true.

Starting from that day, Dora taught her daughter how to communicate with the universe, and the family tradition was allowed to continue.

**MORAL:** You shouldn't forget to dream, both when awake and asleep. When you have a wish, you should put all of your effort into making sure that it comes true.

# Mr. No

Once upon a time, there was a country where all the people were happy and kind, the days were perfect, and life went by in peace and harmony. Well, not quite all the people were like that. Everyone was like that except for one strange and grumpy person, who was unpleasant and asocial. The others called him "Mr. No."

Mr. No was an old man with white and unkempt hair who always wore a dressing gown and slippers. It didn't matter when you met him, he never agreed with anyone or anything, and he always ruined the best of moments with one resounding "no."

"Good morning, here is your mail! Here you go," said the postman with a smile.

"No!" replied Mr. No angrily.

"Then, I'll just leave it inside your mailbox," replied the postman.

"No!" snorted once again the old man.

"It's always the same story every morning! I'm only doing my job as the postman, and to be honest, I don't even understand who would want to write you a letter!" said the postman while going away, still carrying Mr. No's mail.

As the door slammed with a thud, people could hear Mr. No shouting from inside, "No, no, and no! I don't want the mail!" By now, the postman had already left.

While time in the country passed by happily for everyone, Mr. No's life was filled with monotony and solitude. Some people had learned to avoid him in order to avoid ruining their mood. However, others wanted to save him thinking that they could change him, and went to visit him often.

"Good morning, today my help group and I would like to..." a slipper landed on the neighbor's face before she could finish her sentence.

"I already said no!" concluded Mr. No, who had thrown the slipper, and who then slammed the door shut. The lady stayed there staring at the door for a while, and then she left looking unhappy.

The doorbell rang again later that morning. It was an old friend who came with a tomato plant as a present. They had been good friends when they were younger, and the man had never forgotten the good times when Mr. No was different.

"Hey, I was in the area, so I decided to bring you a tomato plant. If you grow this, you will be able to eat its fruits. May I come in?" asked the old friend, offering Mr. No the tomato plant.

Mr. No, without any hesitation, shouted, "No! You can't come in, but the plant could be useful," and after snatching the plant from the farmer's hands, he slammed the door shut and left his friend standing there open-mouthed.

Every morning, the postman returned with a letter in his hand, but he was promptly and rudely told to go away. There was also the priest, the baker, the greengrocer, the gardener and many others who rang Mr. No's bell at least once a week to try to bring happiness to his heart. Nothing seemed to work. Mr. No had changed several years ago, except no one knew why.

One morning like any other, Mr. No's doorbell kept ringing unceasingly. The postman wasn't taking his finger off of the button, and Mr. No was starting to get furious. The postman had a letter open in his hand and continued to ring that doorbell without stopping.

"I decided to open one of your letters!" shouted the postman from Mr. No's garden. "You really need to read this one! It was written by a boy who patiently sends you the same letter every day, but you never read it!"

"No, go away! Besides, you shouldn't read other people's mail!" muttered Mr. No from behind the door.

So, the postman, without any hesitation, started reading the letter out loud. "Dear Mr. No, we moved into this new house a few weeks ago. When we were tidying up the basement, I found an old tin box. The name, "Little Tom," was written on it, and when I opened it..."

All of a sudden, Mr. No's head peeked out of the doorway. The door was only half-open, but something had clearly caught his attention. "Keep on reading!" whispered Mr. No in a quiet but firm voice.

So, the postman continued to read: "As I was saying...when I opened the tin box, I found many pictures. There were two children playing together, on their bikes, skating in the park, having fun on the beach, in the countryside, they seemed to be really good friends..."

Mr. No went out in the garden without saying anything, and sat down on the steps to the porch.

The postman saw him from the corner of his eye, but didn't say anything because he didn't want to ruin the moment, and he continued with: "There weren't only pictures, but also a sling, some circus figurines, colored pins, and a piece of paper with your address written on it as well as a message. If you want to know what the message said, please come see us" the letter ended abruptly like that, and it had an address on it.

Mr. No grabbed the letter from the postman's hands, put on his hat, and got on his bike, saying, "You were right, I should've read that letter!"

When Mr. No knocked on that house's door, which he already knew very well, a boy with his mom opened it, saying, "We were waiting for you. You came to see what that message said, right? Come in, take a seat."

Sitting on the couch, while all the family stared at him, Mr. No had started crying, holding a piece of paper in his hand that said this.

"Dear brother, do you remember our happy times together? Some of our best moments and our favorite games are stored inside this box. I know that we haven't talked in ten long years and I'm very sorry for that. I'm very sorry for what happened, but you will always remain my brother, and the best friend that I have ever had. Even though we didn't talk during these years, I never stopped thinking about you. I will always remember you as the kind and helpful person that you were, and I'm grateful that you were a part of my family."

Then the letter ended with one request. "Whoever finds this box, please deliver it to my brother at this address."

The boy, seeing Mr. No burst into tears, sat next to him and held his hand, and he asked, "This house that we moved into was your brother's, right?"

Mr. No replied that, sometimes in life, you grow distant with some people. After not talking to him for many years, his brother had passed away from old age. Suddenly he realized that he would never have the chance to make up with his brother and that he would never see him again.

He had wasted all those years because of useless arguments. It was such a great shock for Mr. No that he stopped talking to everyone. He became grumpy, and he started saying "no" to anyone who tried to go near him. That explained Mr. No's strange behavior!

Starting from the day he found that box, Mr. No promised that he would never again waste a single day being angry with the world. He had managed to once again become the child whom he used to be, and who really loved games, adventures, other people, and his brother.

**MORAL:** In life, there are times to say both yes and no, but it's important not to overdo it with one of the two. You need to understand when it's time to say yes and when instead it's better to say no.

# The Sorcerer's Amulet

The elves had lived for thousands of years in the greenest part of the jungle without a name. They were the guardians of nature and they lived in harmony with all the other creatures. Their biggest village, "Bivouac," had the most famous school of magic in all the land.

Not only elves, but also fairies, witches, wizards, and pixies came to the school from all over the world to learn the art of magic. The main reason for this was that, among the school's teachers, there was the amazing Cornelius, who was the most powerful wizard to have ever lived. It is said that the most powerful wizards in the world had learned everything from him.

Lilith, born and raised in Bivouac, was the stereotypical lazy elf who, with a lot of difficulty, was forced by his parents to go study at the school of magic to learn from Cornelius. Not only was Lilith lazy, but he was also known as the unlucky elf. Wherever he went, disaster always struck. He had never loved to study nor loved the art of magic, and his favorite hobbies included looking at the sky, eating as much as he could, playing all day, and sleeping.

However, Cornelius had always had a lot of patience for this elf, and people asked themselves why such a clumsy and useless creature studied under such a powerful wizard. Why was he admitted when so few people were lucky enough to receive master Cornelius' teachings?

For example, one time, Lilith destroyed the entire chemistry lab with a single gesture, and another time, he burned down half the swamp while trying to practice fire magic. Another time, he used the wrong spell and put half the school to sleep. This is not to mention that time when he arrived in school with a poisonous mushroom thinking that he had found a rare plant, and instead ended up poisoning a bunch of people. What about that time when they had to fish him out from a group of crocodiles? Luckily, Cornelius was always there to fix the troubles that Lilith caused.

Many students had even started to avoid Lilith, scared that something bad might happen to them. Even though Lilith was a good elf, he was also extremely unlucky, and being near him was more dangerous than provoking a group of angry orcs.

One day, while Lilith was tidying up his notes in the library, Cornelius called him to his office because he wanted to talk to Lilith on his own.

Cornelius started his speech with, "Dear Lilith, I've known you ever since you were a small boy, but recently I've started to become worried. Have you ever wondered why your situation doesn't improve? I would like to do something to help you."

"Are you talking about my bad luck?" asked Lilith.

Cornelius quickly added, "Yours isn't bad luck, it's just lack of confidence. I know for sure that there is infinite potential hidden inside of you. Now, take this, and make sure you always carry it with you." He held out his hand and gave an amulet to the young elf.

"What is this?" asked Lilith.

"This is called a calm stone. It has the power to get rid of negative energy and it can extract hidden potential, but in exchange, you must never tell anyone about it. It was thanks to this stone that I became the most powerful wizard of them all. Now go, and you'll be sure to see great improvements," concluded Cornelius.

Lilith wore the amulet around his neck as if he had just received the most precious treasure of all the seven kingdoms and went back home thinking, "Why did Cornelius give me this treasure? Doesn't he know that I could lose this in a flash? What if I really lose it? He must trust a clumsy elf like me a lot! However, I do feel great tonight. Is it possible that the stone is already having effect?"

The next day, in fact, something strange did happen. Lilith arrived on time to his class and nothing terrible happened all morning. Rather, he seemed more focused than usual. You could see a proud smile on his face, and even he felt that there was something different, but he wasn't quite sure what it was.

In the following days, he started standing out a lot. He shone in his mastery of the various magical arts and he showed great control in his communication with plants. Then, he obtained great results in controlling fire, and he even managed to surpass one of the teachers during a lesson.

He certainly didn't go unnoticed by the school while his shocked classmates couldn't understand how he had changed so much recently. What had happened to Lilith? What had happened to that clumsy elf, who was the unluckiest creature of all the jungle without a name? It seemed that he had suddenly transformed, and the clumsy creature they all knew had been replaced by a powerful elf.

His classmates had started to want to be his friends, and the times when being near him brought lots of trouble seemed to be forgotten.

"Teach me your secret!" asked his jealous classmates.

"Excellent!" exclaimed many teachers.

"We're very proud of you!" said repeatedly his mom and dad.

Lilith, though gladdened by how things were going, still had a weight on his stomach, that he couldn't get rid of.

"If they all knew the secret behind my skills, no one would talk to me anymore!" he thought, dejectedly.

So, one day, after a lesson, he went to the house of Cornelius to confess those sad thoughts that had been in his mind for days.

"Master, I'm here to return the amulet, and I'm grateful for everything you did for me, but I don't have any merit, and I can't keep relying on a stone all my life. It's not right!"

Cornelius burst out laughing, looked at his pupil, and with a serious tone said, "Stone? Amulet? You can't possibly be talking about that piece of glass that you keep inside your necklace, right?"

"Piece of glass?" snorted Lilith, looking at the amulet.

"Exactly! A piece of glass around your neck, nothing more, and nothing less," replied Cornelius.

Then Lilith started to mumble: "But...but...the power of the stone...the amulet that made you extremely powerful?"

"Dear Lilith," cut in Cornelius, throwing the necklace into the fireplace, "sometimes a teacher needs to do all kinds of things in order to give some confidence to his pupils. The stone was just an excuse, and that hidden power was inside of you the whole time. You just didn't know it yet."

**MORAL:** We all have some unique and special skills, we just need to find out what they are and to have some confidence in ourselves.

# The Feather of the Phoenix

Legends tell of a great bird of light called the Phoenix. Famous for its immortality, it rose from the ashes through the millennia. Those who knew how to listen could hear the Phoenix's song at dawn.

This tale had always been told in the Mamba tribe. It had been passed down through so many generations that the Phoenix became the tribe's symbol.

The Mamba were an indigenous people who lived in the valley below the holy mountain, which was called this way because it was the place where the Phoenix had been born.

It was the year when the tribe decided who would be its next chief and according to tradition, the candidates had to face three trials to prove their worth. Both the men, who were strong and brave, and the women, who were clever and wise, could participate in these trials.

In the first trial, the participants had to swim to the big rock without being eaten by the sharks. For the second trial, they had to go without food for two days. For the third one, they had to climb to the top of the mountain, find the flower of Pac, and climb back down without letting a single of its petals fall.

Unfortunately, when the first trial was about to begin, the elderly shaman fell to the ground screaming in pain after being bitten by a scorpion and injected with its powerful venom.

Mandu, her grandson, was participating in the competition, but he abandoned the trials as soon as he found out about the accident, to go see his grandma.

A faint sigh came out of his grandma's lips, "What are you doing here, can't you see that I'm old and dying? No one can save me anymore and you're giving up on the dream of your life to stay here with me. You've always wanted to become the chief of the tribe, right?"

"It's just a stupid trial, grandma and you're much more important," replied Mandu without having any second thoughts. Then, he suddenly had an idea, and turned to his mother, who was looking over his grandma, and shouted, "The Phoenix! That's who could cure grandma! I will go look for her!"

His mother looked at him in amazement, and sighing, said with a weak voice, "Don't be silly, the phoenix doesn't exist. It's just a legend of our village, no one has ever seen her."

However, his grandma, who had very little energy left, managed to whisper something, "The phoenix really exists, but to find her you have to..." and she fell asleep without even finishing her sentence.

Mandu didn't want to listen to any more excuses, and he decided that he would leave immediately, with or without his family's approval. As the legend said, the phoenix could only be seen in one place, the top of the mountain which was also the place where the third trial took place. The mountain was so tall that its summit could be seen from the end of the world, but the path to reach the top was very dangerous.

So, he set off in a hurry without even stocking up on food, and ran to the mountaintop as if possessed by a demon. If he never stopped, he would be able to reach the summit by late at night, and there was no better time to find a bird of light than during the night.

Meanwhile, Bobo, Mandu's older brother, was also participating in the three trials. He wished to be the chief of the tribe so badly, that he even forgot about his own family. Bobo was a mass of muscles, strong as a bear, and fearless as a warrior. He didn't love his brother, and he would've done anything in order to win. He was the first one to return from the big rock of the first trial, and he started fasting.

At the same time, Mandu had gone most of the way up the mountain, but he had also faced many obstacles. Quicksand had delayed him for hours before he could finally free himself. Then, the spiteful monkeys had blocked him, then he had to run away from snakes, all while being on an empty stomach.

So, tired and sore, he finally reached the mountaintop. The view was breathtaking, the air was pure, and there was only silence. The Phoenix, however, was nowhere to be seen, and not even nightfall could reveal the light that he was looking for, and he started to think that he had gone all that way for nothing.

The sun was starting to rise, and by now Mandu had spent two days on top of the mountain, and he didn't even have the strength to return home. "I'm very sorry grandma, but I failed" muttered Mandu weakly, getting ready for the worst.

All of a sudden, a small rock hit his head. The spiteful monkeys had followed him all the way to the top, trying to give him trouble. Another rock was thrown at him, and then another, and then another again.

"Darned heartless monkeys! Can't you see that I can barely stand up? Go away! Shoo! Leave me alone!" Shouted Mandu, trying to scare them.

"Hu-hu, ah-ah-ah!" laughed the satisfied monkeys.

"What do you want? Wasn't that enough?" shouted Mandu.

"Hu-hu, ah-ah-ah," continued the monkeys, jumping madly all over the mountaintop.

Then a rock was suddenly thrown with such strength, that it made Mandu pass out on the spot. At that point, the monkeys, instead of continuing with their game, suddenly ran away as if scared by something.

When Mandu opened his eyes, a blinding light was shining on all the mountaintop, and instead of the monkeys, there was a huge bird with feathers made of fire and a very long tail. He couldn't manage to keep his eyes open for long, and he quickly closed them again, falling asleep with a strange voice in his head, "Drink me, and you will be saved...drink me, and you will be saved."

When Bobo arrived on top of the mountain, he was the first to reach the peak, he had the flower of Pac with him, and he would soon be the chief of the tribe. Surprisingly, he found his brother passed out, without any strength, lying on a rock. Mandu had a red and shiny feather in his hand, and he held it tight while sleeping deeply.

"If I left you here, no one would ever forgive me, so I'll carry you home on my shoulders, after all I'm the tribe chief now, aren't I?" said Bobo proudly. Thus, he put his brother over his shoulders and climbed down the mountain, until he reached the village.

Mandu had by now woken up, and strangely his energy had come back, and he noticed that he was holding a warm feather in his hand.

When he saw the feather, he remembered everything: the monkeys, the blinding light, that strange voice in his head...the Phoenix!

"Drink me, and you will be saved...of course! The feather!" shouted Mandu loudly, and then he practically jumped from his brother's back and ran as fast as he could to his grandma, who didn't have much time left to live.

"Trust me" said Mandu, making tea with the feather, which lay at the bottom of the cup. Then he made his grandma drink it, holding her head with his hand.

Everyone was shocked when the old shaman suddenly jumped on her feet with her eyes wide open, as if reborn, and full of energy. As she looked around her in disbelief, she pointed at her grandson Mandu and shouted from the bottom of her lungs, "You found the Phoenix!" His grandma was safe and sound.

A week later, the ceremony to elect the new tribe chief took place, and Bobo was shocked when the village elders nominated Mandu as the new chief instead of him.

"You showed that you have courage, you showed that you're strong, and most of all, you didn't abandon your family. Family is more important than the desire for power, and a man who risks everything for his own family has the right qualities to become the chief" explained one of the elders.

"May the Phoenix be with you, Mandu!" they all shouted together. The Mamba tribe had found its new leader.

**MORAL:** Even though, sometimes, you might have to give up on some things in order to take care of your family, you must remember that you do it because family is the most important thing there is.

# Molly's Dream

On a Saturday, in the afternoon, Molly came home from school and ran to her room looking sad. She knew that this wasn't a day like any other, but instead, it was the last day she would spend in this house that she loved. On the next day, all of her family would move to another city and Molly couldn't accept that she would have to say goodbye to all her friends. So, she took her bag off and tried to sneak out on her tiptoes hoping that no one would hear her.

Right before she could go out, though, her mom stopped her, raised an eyebrow, and started to scold her.

"Where do you think you're going, young lady? You know that today is a very important day, right?" said her mom with a firm tone, surprising Molly who was already in the doorway.

"But mom, I really wanted to..." Molly was quickly interrupted.

"No buts, young lady, get to work! First, do your homework, and then pack up your suitcase. You will have some time left to go say goodbye to your friends after."

So Molly, resigned, went to her room to pack up her things. After all, she didn't want to disappoint her mom.

"I will just rest for five minutes on the couch before starting" declared Molly, with a yawn, and she fell asleep in no time with her head on the pillow.

"Psst... hey! Wake up... come on!" whispered a voice that she didn't know.

Molly jumped onto her feet. "Who are you? And what are you doing in my room? Wait, this isn't my room! Where am I?" asked Molly, starting to feel lost.

"Go....we need to go! Don't think! You think too much and I want to go!" replied a man with a long and white dress who was wearing a donut-shaped hat on his head. Then, he added, "you always dream about me... but you never remember me! How rude! Some people call me "the man of sleep," others call me "Morpheus," but you may call me "man of the dreams," and now it's late. So, let's take a shortcut."

Then, all of a sudden, a huge chasm opened below them and the two fell into a tunnel that looked like it was made of water, and then landed on a soft floor made of bouncy rubber. When Molly stopped screaming and opened her eyes, she realized that she was alone.

"So, am I dreaming? And to think that I wanted to do my homework" snorted Molly, who was a bit calmer now.

"Did she say do homework?" A voice came out from behind a tree that looked like it was made of paper.

"She said just that! Ha-ha-ha-ha!" Replied another voice from the opposite side.

Two strange cats walked up to the girl. One was tall and thin with yellow stripes, the other was fat and short with very long fur.

"What is it that you have to do that's so important?" asked one of the cats.

"I need to pack my suitcase, and then I need to finish studying," snorted once again Molly, shaking off the strange blue petals that covered her whole dress.

"She said study! Ha-ha-ha-ha!" The fat cat fell down rolling.

"Oh, for heaven's sake! What are you two laughing at?" grumbled Molly.

"No no no, they're already waiting for you, we need to go! Hurry!" replied the thin cat, and he took the girl by one hand and dragged her towards a strange bridge that looked like a rainbow.

"Eat a bit of it! Color is good for the skin!" shouted one of the cats. Then, while he walked away with his partner, he added, "Remember that they're waiting for you! Reach the end of the rainbow, and then turn right four times until you're back where you started. Is everything clear?"

Molly hadn't understood much, but she still followed the strange directions. She thus walked until she reached a lake that seemed frozen, except that it wasn't cold at all.

"You can walk on water too if you want! See? I always walk on it!" shouted a panda who had come out of nowhere.

Then, he also said, "Do you see all those people in the middle of the lake? They're waiting for you there. Come with me, let's go!"

Molly couldn't stop looking at her surroundings, so beautiful was the scenery she was seeing. There were mushrooms the size of mountains, all bright, the sky was of a red-gold color, and the trees were walking around looking very busy. Floating in the air, there were many fluffy white things that tasted like sugar, and strange animals ran around in all directions, looking like they were having a lot of fun.

In the middle of the frozen lake, all of Molly's friends were there to welcome her. They had prepared a delicious buffet and splendid music accompanied the food.

"My friends! What are you doing here?" shouted Molly.

"What do you mean, what are we doing here? We're here to say goodbye! That's why we're here! Don't make that sad face!" said one of her friends, and he grabbed a star from the sky, held it between his fingers, and put it inside a pocket in Molly's skirt.

"I can't stop being sad, because I will never see you again!" cried Molly, whose tears, instead of falling on her cheeks, seemed to float in the air, going up towards the sky.

"Dear Molly, today is an important day, and it's the perfect day to grow up a little. We will always be with you, and when you miss us, all you have to do is come see us in your dreams" chorused her friends.

The party continued with songs and dancing, with happiness and laughter, with fireworks and live music. Molly felt her heart beating fast, and at the same time felt incredibly happy. She wished that day would never end. Right when she was having the most fun, someone grabbed her by the shoulder and called her name, and the frozen lake suddenly melted, and Molly fell in the water together with everyone else.

"Molly! Wake up! Young lady, it's time to wake up!" shouted her mom, shaking her by the shoulder.

"I had a dream mom, and all my friends were there" stammered Molly while she opened her eyes. Then she hugged her mom and said, "I'm not afraid of moving anymore, mom. I know that all my friends will always be here with me in any moment."

"I'm proud of you, my dear. You'll see that we will all love the new city! Now let's go, because they're all waiting for you!" said her mom happily.

"Who is waiting for me?" asked Molly.

Her mom gave her a big smile and then she put her mouth on her daughter's ear, whispering, "All your friends came to visit you, there's a party in your honor downstairs in the living room! Come on...let's go!"

**MORAL:** Friends come and go, but real friends stay with you forever. You need to keep those close and take good care of them. There will always be chances to make new friends in life, though.

# The Princess and the Promise to the Giant

Once upon a time there was a castle near a forest, far from the city, in a quiet and lonely place.

The richest family of the country lived in that castle, the king, the queen, and the princess Asia. Just outside the castle lived the soldiers as well as many servants, tireless workers at the service of their king.

Asia loved walking through the nearby forest, but she wasn't allowed to go out on her own, since the princess' life was very precious, so she always had to be accompanied by some guards.

Soon, Asia would have to get married and replace her mom as the queen of her country.

Asia wasn't like every other princess, and instead of spending her days in court, she preferred to sneak out of the castle and have fun adventures in nature. She loved to gather wild fruits, flowers, and herbs which she often used to make desserts, since she liked eating sweet things.

When she climbed down the tower's stairs in secret, in order to go out, she always wore rags so that no one would recognize her. This way, she managed to hide her real identity.

However, one day, since she couldn't find her favorite berries, she decided to have a walk in the wood. After walking for a while, she discovered a secret garden full of fruit trees, berries, nuts, and everything else that someone could possibly want from nature.

"I've never seen so much fruit before! Why is there such a beautiful garden in the middle of the forest?" exclaimed Asia enthusiastically.

Without thinking about it too much, she started to gather as many things as she could fit in the bag on her shoulders, even though a lot of the food actually ended up in her tummy because of how delicious it was. Continuing her walk, she realized that where the garden ended, there was a huge house.

"It looks like an abandoned house! Maybe I'll be able to find something rare inside!" said Asia a little anxiously when she was about to go inside the house.

Surprisingly, the princess instead found a clean and tidy house. The strangest thing about it was that it was all so big and out of proportion that it made her feel very small.

"Look at this huge table! Look at this furniture! I've never seen chairs this tall before! Even the bed is huge!" she shrieked excitedly.

In just a second, her face suddenly changed when she found herself in front of what seemed to be an angry giant, a creature so tall and so big that it made the huge house look perfectly normal.

"Who told you that you could come in? Who told you that you could eat the fruits of my garden?" asked the giant with a huge and scary voice.

Asia was paralyzed with fear. This time she was in big trouble, and she didn't even have any of her guards. She was alone and in danger. The giant then delicately grabbed the princess, put her on top of the large table, and started to examine her.

He hit his chest with his hands and announced with a firm voice, "very well, my little thief! You will pay for everything that you stole! You will stay here with me and be my servant for as long as I need you!"

"Sorry, I can't be your servant. I'm a princess, and I have never been anyone's servant, and I never will be!" replied Asia, who was a bit offended.

"You...a princess? Ha ha ha ha! Have you seen yourself in the mirror?" laughed the giant, with the hands on his belly. "Listen here, little human, you can pretend to be anyone you want, but I won't care! From now on, you belong to me! Now get to work, make me dinner!" commanded the giant.

Asia was tied and forced to take care of all the housework without being able to complain. Many days went by and the castle was filled with confusion. The princess had disappeared and all the king's soldiers were desperately looking for her.

One evening, while Asia was being forced to clean, the giant started drinking alcohol until he couldn't control himself well anymore. In fact, he could barely stand up on his feet, and he couldn't think very clearly.

The princess decided to take advantage of this, to try to convince the giant that she didn't belong here. "You see, by now all the castle will be looking for me, and if they find me here in your house, you will definitely be in trouble!"

"I've never seen someone who was so bad at housework before, it's like you've never held a broom in your hands before!" said the giant, crying.

"I...I've never ever held a broom in my hands before! I'm a princess, so I never took care of housework!" shouted Asia, twirling a dirty piece of cloth in her hand. "Let's make a deal. If you free me now, I promise that I will return and I'll bring my servants here to you, and they will take care of everything for a whole year!"

The giant, who was now struggling to keep his eyes open, barely had the energy to sit in his chair, but curious, he asked, "Are they any good at least?"

"They're the best of all the kingdom!" the princess stated proudly. "Not only that, but I will also give you some small fruit trees that you can add to your garden!"

The giant didn't think twice about it since he was so drunk, and he freed the princess and told her to hurry up. "Be quick, though, and bring me some cheese too! I love cheese!" he replied with a very sleepy voice, and his eyes had by now completely closed.

Asia was finally free from slavery, and she ran as fast as she could through the forest, going back the same way she had come. When she arrived at the castle, she was in such a sorry state that the guards barely recognized her.

In the castle, everyone gathered for a special event. The king and the queen wanted to give a party to celebrate the return of their beloved daughter, who was safe and sound and who had brought back peace to the castle. A feast was prepared, and even the soldiers and the servants were invited to it. They all celebrated for a whole day.

When the giant woke up and became sober again, he realized that he had made a huge mistake to trust that wretch, "I fell for a fake promise! I've been tricked!" he shouted furiously. "I will never ever again believe what a human being says!"

After a week, the giant was forced to take those words back because three horse-drawn carriages appeared in his garden. A beautiful woman came out of one of these carriages. She had a dress that touched the ground and she brought gifts.

A servant made an announcement, "Ladies and gentlemen, bow in the presence of princess Asia!"

The princess, with one gesture, gave the order to start unloading the carriages: "Dear giant, as promised, I brought everything that you wanted and even more! I admit that I made a mistake, by eating your food without your permission, so let me repair my error."

The giant had never seen so many provisions in his life before; there was plenty of cheese, fruit trees, bags of flour, corn, and many bottles of wine.

"These people will take care of your house for quite some time. Take good care of them, give them a warm place to live in, and give them all the food that they need. Remember that they must never be tied up or forced to do anything they don't want to!"

Then she added, "from now on, my kingdom won't have servants anymore and they will become free people instead. They will be able to decide whether they want to stay with you or not. This will be up to them, and you will have to accept their decision."

Not only had the princess kept her promise, but she had also learned what it meant to be humble, how difficult a servant's life was, and how lonely a giant in the middle of the forest could get.

From that day onwards, whoever worked in the castle was called a worker and was paid for his services.

**MORAL:** Every creature has the right to decide what they want to do and what they don't. No one should be forced to do anything.

# The Nut Robbers

A family had lived for many generations in a quiet mansion in the countryside, and inside this house, there was another much smaller house where another family of tiny creatures lived.

The humans who lived in the mansion, called them the nut robbers. They were named like this because they loved all kinds of nuts. The humans didn't really believe in this and they thought that it was just a family legend. In fact, when things disappeared from the house, especially food, they always blamed mice.

However, the nut robbers really did exist, and they lived in a tiny house that was found in the humans' basement. The nut robbers were just like the humans except much smaller. These tiny creatures had adapted to survive by borrowing things from the humans.

Buttons, pins, pieces of wood, and fragments of tiles all became part of their house which they had carefully built, making sure that they were never found out. This way, they could continue taking human food leftovers without ever worrying about running out of things to eat.

One day, however, Pangu, the son of the nut robber family, had an unexpected event. The human family had bought a cat, hoping to get rid of the mice stealing their food.

Pangu was putting a piece of cheese in his bag, feeling safe because the humans weren't currently at home. Suddenly, a furry monster appeared out of nowhere, and it didn't seem to have good intentions.

Pangu ran away as fast as he could. The cheese was weighing him down, and he certainly didn't expect to run into a cat, the number one enemy of the nut robbers. He couldn't manage to reach the basement, so he had to hide in one of the rooms upstairs.

He had just broken his parents' rule. Never go into the rooms upstairs.

The cat carefully sniffed the air, looking for clues, and quickly found the nut robber. With a feline jump, he threw himself onto the poor Pangu, who just barely managed to reach a half-opened door, which he quickly entered.

He bumped into a very hard thing. He had run into Glen's foot, the young daughter of the humans. With all that confusion, he hadn't realized that they had all come back home.

When Glen saw that small creature who was being chased by the cat, she immediately closed the door and picked up Pangu with her hands. "Please don't eat me! I'm not tasty! I bet that you wouldn't even be able to digest me!" shouted Pangu, who was panicking.

"You're a nut robber, right?" asked Glen, as if she knew everything about them, when it was actually the first time that she saw one. Then, she put little Pangu on the table and said, "I wonder what mom and dad will say, if I tell them about you!"

"Please don't tell anyone that you saw me, or else me and my family will be in trouble!" explained Pangu with a shaky voice.

Suddenly, someone knocked on the door. It was Glen's mom who came in without waiting for a reply, and Glen, quick as a flash, hid the nut robber behind her back.

"Is everything all right, dear?" asked her mom, a little suspiciously.

"Everything is fine! I'll finish my homework, and then come down for dinner mom!"

Now they were alone again, and Pangu felt safe by now. He realized that he could still get out of this mess.

"My name is Pangu, and I live with my family down in the basement. We always come out at night, or when you humans are outside so that we are never seen" said the little creature.

"You're safe with me, Pangu, now calm down. However, if my parents saw you, then I'm not sure what would happen! I don't even want to imagine what would happen if the cats found you!" said Glen, worriedly.

"Cats? Are you telling me that that furry monster outside isn't alone?" asked Pangu.

"Sadly no, mom and dad bought three of them and not only that, they also got some professionals who are experts at catching mice." Then, she explained that she would soon go live with her mom in another city while her dad would stay there with the cats.

"Mom and dad said that they need a break, so I'll go live with mom for a while."

Then, Pangu came down from the palm of Glen's hand and said nervously, "If what you say is true, then we can't live in this house anymore. I have to warn my parents!"

Glen accompanied him to the basement's door, making sure that none of the cats were following them.

When the small nut robber returned home and explained what had happened to his parents, a heavy mood came over the house, and everyone became very worried about the situation. Mom and dad were scared that they would end up as all nut robbers do when humans discover them, captured and then kicked out of the house, or even worse, eaten alive by cats.

"We won't be able to move freely anymore if three cats are hunting for us!" exclaimed Pangu's mom.

Pangu's dad decided to say, "We will need to change home again! This one isn't safe anymore. For now, we'll think of a plan, and in the meantime, we'll use up our supplies, so that we won't have to go out again for a few days."

A few days passed, and it was time for Glen and her mom to move out. Glen, who hadn't been able to see her little friend again, secretly went down to the basement to look for him.

In the meantime, the nut robbers were packing up their things, forced to look for a new place. Suddenly the roof of their house was lifted: some pieces of the wall came off, and they fell into the nut robbers' living room, who all hid under the table out of fear.

It was Glen who was looking for them, and she had managed to find their tiny house which looked a lot like her own dollhouse.

Pangu stood up on his feet and said, "Mom.... Dad, meet my new human friend, Glen". His mother almost fainted from fear.

Glen gestured to be quiet, and then she whispered quietly, "I won't leave you here, you're not safe! Let me bring you away with me. You'll be able to live in our new home which doesn't have any cats!".

So, after Glen's mom had put everything in the car, they left for their new home a bit melancholic. Glen's mom never found out that the nut robbers' family was traveling with them inside the dollhouse among her daughter's things.

**MORAL:** Even creatures smaller than us deserve our attention and our respect.

# Lilly and the Monster on the Bed

Every house has a monster, whether you believe it or not, and their greatest passion is to scare children.

Momo wasn't a monster like any other. He didn't like hiding inside wardrobes or under beds, nor did he like scaring children. Momo only had one dream, a bed all for himself where he could sleep and a child for a friend. So, he began visiting all the children's houses, but often they were already taken by another monster who lived inside the wardrobe or under the bed.

"Go away! This room is already mine!" shouted the monsters when they saw Momo come in, trying to drive him away.

Momo always replied, "I'm only looking for a comfortable bed to sleep in. I don't want to scare children. I love children!"

The monsters always ended up laughing loudly, amused by how strange Momo was. "Are you crazy or what? Ha ha ha ha, I can't believe you actually said that!"

Momo wondered if he would ever find a place where he belonged and asked himself why he should behave like everyone else wanted just because he was a monster. One day, in a house that looked like every other, something different happened.

Momo found a bedroom full of drawings of a monster with only one tooth and one eye who seemed very evil. A little girl called Lilly slept in that bedroom. Well, actually, rather than sleep, she spent every night awake under the sheets with a flashlight, scared that the monster with one tooth and one eye would come back.

As soon as Momo came in, the wardrobe opened, and a big voice whispered, trying not to make too much noise, "can't you see that this room is already taken? Find a place of your own, this room belongs to me! You can either leave or run here inside the wardrobe together with me and wait for the best moment to scare her!"

Momo, who was also whispering, replied, "No thanks."

"No? Why not?" replied the monster in the wardrobe.

"Wardrobes are too small and dark, so I definitely don't want to go inside one." explained Momo.

The monster with one eye quickly whispered, "Then go under the bed but hurry up before she wakes up!".

Momo looked under the bed and said, "Under the bed, there's so much dust, too many toys, and it's uncomfortable too! Why would I ever hide there? I want to stay on top of it!"

"On top of the bed?" said the monster with one eye who couldn't believe what he was hearing. "I must have too much fur in my ears. I'm not sure that I heard right. Did you really say that you want to stay on the bed?"

"Indeed, I did. I'm not a monster, I'm Momo, and I don't want to scare anyone!" replied Momo.

So, the monster with one eye burst out laughing, "Ha ha ha ha! Now I've heard everything, you crazy monster, you useless pile of fur! What do you even do in life, then?"

Meanwhile, they hadn't realized that Lilly was awake and had been listening to them. She had covered her whole body and face to her cheeks with the duvet, and you could only see her eyes peeking out. She gathered her courage, and, turning towards Momo, she said, "The bed next to mine has always been empty, and you can sleep here whenever you want, but only if you promise to never ever scare me. Mom and dad won't even realize that you're there. They can never see monsters, maybe because they're too busy"

So, from that day onwards, Momo found a bed to sleep in as well as a friend to talk to. The monster with one eye and one tooth was forced to leave that house, saddened that he couldn't scare Lilly anymore who felt safe, protected by her new roommate, Momo. It's better to have a monster as a friend than as an enemy!

**MORAL:** To get over a fear, we just have to become friends with it!

# The Desert Caravan

Once upon a time, there was a desert divided in half, and each half was ruled by a different king.

This desert had once been a green valley, but almost all the plants died because of twenty years of drought, and they were replaced by earth and sand.

One of the two kings was called Tulio. He was known as a very sociable and altruistic person, and he cared about his people and about all of his lands.

The other ruler, Kato, was instead feared by everyone. He was very dishonest, and he never shared anything with anyone. Indeed, the people of his kingdom lived a life of hardship, and many were enslaved and barely had anything to eat.

Kato made money by looting other kingdoms and by sending his guards to rob rich merchants who passed through the desert, and he kept everything he stole for himself.

On the other hand, Tulio ensured that his people could live a noble and dignified life, but despite his efforts, the drought in the valley kept getting worse, and food was starting to run out.

Tulio decided that it was time to do something in order to save his people. So he decided to visit an old friend who ruled over the green forest, traveling on camels together with all his guards.

Once they arrived, the ruler of the forest welcomed Tulio into his palace and asked to know the whole story.

"Ever since our climate changed, our harvests slowly got worse and worse, and the amount of food decreased, and the people's health declined!" Tulio explained sadly. Then, he continued, "My dear old friend who lives in this beautiful forest, please tell me your secret and help my people. I'll do anything you want in exchange!"

So, the king of the forest replied, "my friend, I'm always happy to help you because I will never forget when you helped me many years ago!"

Having said that, he prepared a caravan full of gold, food supplies, and gave Tulio a small gift.

"Don't ever tell anyone else what I just told you, just follow my instructions and you'll see that things will get better," said the lord of the forest.

Thus, they started traveling with the caravan. The road was long, and Tulio knew well that they would have to be careful. This road was where Kato's bandits attacked rich merchants, stealing everything they could.

Tulio's guards had been warned about this, and they knew that their job was to protect the king and the caravan. It wasn't the first time that they had to deal with the desert bandits. The two kingdoms were next to each other and they had fought many times before.

As they traveled away from the forest kingdom, the vegetation grew sparser and the suffocating heat increased. They had now reached the desert, and they knew that this was where trouble would start.

In fact, king Kato had been informed by a spy that Tulio and his guards were coming back home to their kingdom with a caravan full of gold and supplies. He had even heard that, inside the caravan, there was a solution to their problem which the king of the forest had kindly given to Tulio.

One night, while they were camped below a big rock, the caravan was attacked. Kato's bandits made a surprise attack, trying to steal all the goods. Luckily, some men were on guard duty, and after a short fight, the bandits were forced to run away, but not empty handed. They had managed to steal a few bags of gold.

"King Tulio, we're all fine, but they managed to steal some of the gold!" said one of the guards.

"Don't worry about it, it's fine," replied the king.

The caravan continued down the path which was slowly becoming more arid. There was still a long way to go before they arrived home and they were all a bit nervous.

One morning, while they were crossing a bridge, the bandits prepared an ambush, and some of the guards were hurt, but nothing terrible happened, except that many of the food supplies were stolen.

"King Tulio, the guards who were hurt are fine, but we lost almost all the food" declared a guard.

"Don't worry about it, it's fine" replied the king.

When they had almost reached their kingdom, the caravan was attacked one last time: it was once again the bandits, who never seemed to give up. So, a few more guards were hurt, nothing serious, but this time all the gold was stolen.

"King Tulio, they've practically stolen everything! What a disaster!" shouted a guard.

"Don't worry about it, it's fine," replied the king.

"This is fine? How can you be so calm, my king? What was the purpose of all this trip?" asked the guard.

"I'm calm and anyway, we're all fine right? That's what matters!" declared the king.

When they finally arrived home safe and sound, the caravan was basically empty, but king Tulio's pockets weren't. He took out of them a canvas bag tied with string, and spilled its contents onto one of his hands. The guards watched in amazement: Tulio had many seeds on the palm of his hand, and he ordered to plant them throughout all their valley.

Meanwhile, Kato sat triumphantly on his throne with his loot, satisfied with what he had stolen, and happy to have won once again. He hadn't really understood what was so important about that caravan, what was supposed to solve all their problems, but he didn't care anyway.

However, he hadn't thought about one thing. All that gold couldn't buy anything in that area. You had to travel for a whole month to see any markets. On the other hand, the food would someday run out, and he would have to stock up on it again and again.

A year went by, and many things changed. While Kato's people lived in great poverty, something was changing in Tulio's kingdom. Where there once was desert, all kinds of plants were starting to grow such as palm trees, fruit trees and vegetables.

The valley had become paradise on earth, and it had never been so green, even in ancient times. The people didn't suffer anymore, and many started to trade and sell the fruits of the earth. In fact, Tulio's kingdom became much richer from the sale of food and cloth, which they got from the plants.

It had become the only place in the whole desert where you could restock your supplies and buy things. So, travelers who were going through the desert would often stop in that valley to buy supplies.

One day a guard, who remembered the trip with the caravan that had been looted, told Tulio, "king Tulio, I think I now understand why you weren't worried during the trip. The real treasure we were carrying wasn't the gold or the food. It was the seeds!"

So, Tulio smiled and said, "that's right, the king of the forest predicted that we would be attacked by Kato, and if Kato had known what the real treasure was, then the seeds would've never reached my kingdom!"

Then, he concluded with, "the seeds that my friend gave me can grow even in very hot places and with very little water. Amazing! Don't you think?"

From that day on, even Kato had to buy supplies from Tulio in order to survive, and so he had to spend all the gold he had stolen to buy food.

**MORAL:** The thing that glitters isn't always the most valuable one. Sometimes, even the simplest one has the power to become the most profitable in the end.

# Saba's Travels

In a peaceful neighborhood, in the suburbs of a big city, there lived a young man called Saba, together with his family.

His parents had humble jobs, with which they had bought a humble house, to live in a humble neighborhood, to live a humble life, with a humble car and a humble garden. Everything was so humble, that Saba couldn't accept it.

Saba was by now old enough to understand how the world worked, and often he didn't like what he saw. In fact, he only had one thought in his head. He was very jealous of other people's lives and he spent every day complaining about what he was missing.

He suffered when he went to school because everyone seemed to be better than him. Some were taller, some skinnier, some had a cuter girlfriend, some had a faster motorbike, and so on and so forth.

When he went to the city to do shopping, it was the same. The other houses were bigger and prettier, the gardens were greener and had more flowers, and there were swimming pools. Saba had always dreamed of owning a swimming pool, but his dream hadn't come true yet.

Then, Saba found a job, but his situation didn't change much. He didn't earn as much as the others, he wasn't as clever as the others, and he didn't receive enough compliments.

One day his father, who was fed up with all these complaints, called his son and said, "dear Saba, you've now grown up, and I think that it's time for you to see what the world is like!" exclaimed his father.

"Go to Africa and get to know the poor neighborhoods. Stay there for as long as you need, and then when you come back, tell me what you saw."

So, Saba set out on a journey, going through many countries, and he found out about poverty from a new perspective. He spoke with many people and observed what kind of life they led. He crossed seas and mountains, rivers and lakes, and after three years he finally came back home.

"My dear son, it's been so long!" shouted his father excitedly. Then he asked with a lot of curiosity, "so? How did it go? What did you see?".

"I lived in real poverty, in wooden shacks, and I suffered from hunger and cold. The thing that surprised me the most of these places was that some people who didn't have anything, spent their time being jealous of those who had a little more than them."

"Very well my son, now go to Asia, and explore the wealthy neighborhoods. Stay there for as long as you need and then when you come back, tell me what you saw!"

So, Saba immediately picked up his bags and went to explore new countries. He got to know very educated people, he visited some very nice houses, and he observed how the locals lived. He crossed seas and mountains, rivers and lakes, and after another three years he finally came back home.

"You've grown so much Saba, come here and let me hug you!" said his father, happy to see him again. Then he asked with a lot of curiosity, "so? How did it go? What did you see?"

Saba started to tell his story. "I lived in beautiful houses and I got to know wealthy people. The thing that surprised me the most was that some people who didn't need anything spent their time being jealous of those who had the same things, except a little more expensive."

Then, his father replied, "excellent! I see that you had fun! Now, travel in America and get to know the neighborhoods of the richest people. Stay there for as long as you need and then when you come back, tell me what you saw."

So, Saba grabbed his bags again and flew to America. He started working for rich men, lived in luxurious mansions with swimming pools, and observed how people lived. He crossed seas and mountains, rivers and lakes, and after another four years he finally came back home.

"My beloved son! Welcome home! So? How did it go? What did you see?"

Saba then told his story. "I lived in gigantic mansions with swimming pools and I got to know extremely rich people, and I even got a girlfriend! The thing that surprised me most was that even there, the people who had so much, ended up being jealous of those who had even more!"

Thus, his father said, "Very well! Then, what did you learn from all this?"

"I learned that it doesn't matter where I live, how I live, or how many things I own, if I spend my time thinking about what I don't have, then nothing will ever be enough for me!"

"Excellent!" said his father, "and what else did you learn?"

Saba went on, "I learned five languages, I learned to travel, I found out what love is, I bought a house, and now I have friends all over the world!"

His father immediately replied, "I'm jealous of you now! Look at how many things you did and how many things you learned in your life!" they ended up laughing together.

Then Saba added, smiling, "I missed my family, the house where I was born, the neighborhood, my friends, and I think that in the end I always had everything I needed, but I never realized that."

On that day, his father realized that his son had become a man. Saba had learned to appreciate what he had always had, whereas before he had to go away from his home in order to understand its real value.

**MORAL:** In life, there will always be someone who makes us feel like we're less worthy than them or we might feel badly that we don't own as many things as them. If we stop focusing on other people, we can understand that our happiness only depends on us and on what we think of ourselves. We can bring our own attention back to ourselves.

# The Ecological Idea

Once upon a time, there was a small village near the sea in the middle of clean and uncontaminated nature.

Only one thousand people lived in this village. Each one of them had built a house for themselves or for their own family and they all ate the fruits that they grew, thanks to mother nature's generosity. There were all kinds of crops, many fruit trees, and the sea provided plenty of fish as well as delicious algae.

Every house had a lot of space and a nice garden where its inhabitants could keep their own animals and grow whatever crops they needed. When people wanted to travel, they went on foot, on a horse, or on a bicycle.

The air was extremely clean, breathing was a pleasure, plants grew abundantly wherever you looked, and the sea was a mass of sparkling blue water.

Months went by, years went by, and the number of villagers kept increasing because they lived well there and had many children. Even the number of houses increased since the people needed more space, and so the village grew into a small town.

Many more years went by, and the small town grew so much that it became a city bustling with people. The number of inhabitants eventually became quite large and they didn't all know each other anymore as they used to many years ago.

Then, one day, someone invented cars with which you could travel much faster and without much effort, but at a cost. These machines needed fuel to work, and you had to take that away from nature. Cars also gave out toxic gases that mixed with the air and polluted it.

The years went by, and the city became bigger and bigger, and then one day someone had the smart idea of inventing a system to light the streets and the houses at night. Thus, electricity and electrical lights were born.

This too had a price. To produce energy, they had to use carbon and petroleum which are found in nature. This hurt the environment around the city. By now, all the citizens wanted electricity and few of them cared about how it was produced.

Many years went by, and plastic was invented, which you could use to build any kind of thing from the smallest to the biggest. People used plastic for daily things, and many of these could only be used one time, then they had to be thrown away.

At this point, the city had become gigantic. The houses had turned into very tall palaces where people lived in tiny spaces. There were millions of inhabitants who used cars and electricity every day and threw away a huge amount of plastic, which was used to package food.

You may not believe this, but food started to be wrapped inside plastic bags and sold in places made of iron and cement called supermarkets. This was a huge change, considering that people before just had to go to a farmer to get some food.

The city had become a complete disaster. Pollution from the cars had turned the air gray and people couldn't breathe well anymore. Many roads had been built which the people used to go to work, and they stayed at workplaces all day!

Work was also a strange thing that humans invented many many years ago. It meant toiling all day in exchange for a little money. You had to spend most of your time away from your family, and you lost out on life a bit. However, it was also thanks to work that everyone was able to bring home some food to eat, so it was important.

The car drivers had to put up with the same thing every day and they were furious.

"Come on! Hurry up, or I'll be late!"

"I can't stand all this traffic anymore!"

"I don't want to go to work!"

They had to cut down many trees and free up a lot of space in nature to produce more electrical energy and the amount of vegetation decreased every day.

That's without even mentioning all the plastic and the garbage that by now filled all the streets of the city, since there were many rude people who threw everything on the floor without worrying too much about consequences.

Even the sea, which before had been sparkling blue, had by now been reduced to a big brown puddle full of garbage and filth, which all came directly from the river.

The situation had become unacceptable, but luckily some people were already thinking of a way to fix this situation. A group of scientists had come up with a way to stop using all these materials which were damaging to the environment.

"Finally! I think that I found a solution!" shouted one of them. "Listen to me!"

They started discussing something in a very serious and professional manner.

"Of course! It's just like you say! If we use this method, we can still make it!" shouted another scientist.

"Now, we just need someone who will believe in us!" said another one.

They had discovered that, using energy from the sun, wind and water, they could have the same technologies, but without pollution. They had even found a solution for all that plastic.

So, the scientists contacted all the famous people who had a lot of power in the city and carefully explained their solution.

It wasn't easy at all in the beginning. No one wanted to accept their crazy idea, and many people were too busy to think about the future.

"You want to make cars move with energy from the sun? That's ridiculous!"

"Are you telling me that we can create electricity with water? Are you kidding me?"

"Replace the plastic with a different material that doesn't create pollution? Go away! I don't have time to waste on this!"

As the years went by, though, things changed and more and more people became interested in these revolutionary ideas. Many businessmen managed to profit from this clean energy. Thanks to this, the scientists were able to start building those new technologies.

It took decades before all the population started taking these things seriously. After all this pollution and filth, the city was finally ready to use those new technologies that everyone was talking about.

Not only did they work perfectly, but they also brought lots of advantages to everyone. The city changed considerably and the people started being more careful about their behaviors. The sea slowly became clean again, and many trees were also planted, so the forest became greener than ever.

Cars still existed, but the new ones only worked with solar power, and this made the sky much less gray. The citizens could finally breathe clean air.

**MORAL:** Everything that we do has an effect on nature and ourselves. If we learn to think carefully about our decisions and their consequences in the future, we will be able to make wiser choices. When possible, we should try to save water and electricity. We should also try to take actions that cause the least damage possible to the environment.

## Thank you for purchasing this book!

In the next page, there will be a fun imagination exercise, which will teach you to create your own story!

## Did you like the book? Share your opinion by leaving an honest review on Amazon.

This small effort would help us a lot, and it would also make it more likely that another book with new stories will be published.

Reviews are very important because they show other people that you liked our work. That's why we need your support!

It's a simple and fast action that would only take a minute of your time.

# How to Invent a Little Story

Before leaving you, I'd like to show you a fun game you can do:

This is a stress-free exercise. There are no special rules, you don't have to be in a hurry, and you won't be graded or judged. You will be the inventor and your imagination will be your engine.

You can get inspiration from my ideas, but at the same time, feel free to do whatever you want and remember to use your own imagination! Even a very short story will be good enough to start with, and you'll improve as you invent more!

1 - Take a blank piece of paper and a pen.

2 - Write down the names of your favorite characters that you met in the stories you just read.

3 - Imagine something happening to those characters.

Example:

An unexpected event

A sudden journey

Great curiosity

The arrival of a particular person

4 - Imagine what would happen next.

Example:

What caused the unexpected event?

Did someone leave on that journey?

Does someone want to satisfy their curiosity?

What happened after that particular person arrived?

5 - Find a way to solve their problem or to continue the story. Add another character or two if necessary.

Example:

How did the characters fix the unexpected event?

What did the characters who left on that journey do?

How did they manage to satisfy their curiosity?

How did meeting this particular person go?

6 - Write down the story using only your imagination, but ask for help if you need it.

7 – Think of a nice happy ending, to end the story.

8 - Add a lovely drawing that describes the story.

9 - Sign your work of art with your name.

10 – Now, read it to mom and dad! Maybe they'll be the ones to fall asleep this time!

Repeat as often as you want.

You just became a writer! Congratulations!

## Conclusion

Dear little boys and little girls,

We have reached the end of this beautiful journey made up of magical stories and fantastical words. We have met many odd characters and we have also learned some values that will be useful in life.

By the way, have any of you been able to read the stories on your own? A story can be read many times, and you'll notice that with every re-read it will get easier, I promise!

For the youngest: Have mom and dad read the stories well to you or did your grandparents and uncles read them for you?

I hope I've been able to make you smile and to give you lots of good feelings, but be careful, they could be contagious!

I wish you all lots of magic!

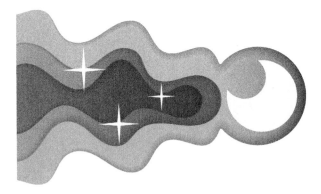

Printed in Great Britain
by Amazon

81477717R00071